POPULAR REWARDS

Flomper and the Flyaway Fairies

and other stories

Award Publications Limited

With thanks to Elizabeth Dale.

ISBN 978-1-78270-144-6

Copyright © Award Publications Limited
Popular Rewards ® is a registered trademark of
Award Publications Limited

First published by Award Publications Limited 2016

Published by Award Publications Limited,
The Old Riding School, Welbeck,
Worksop, S80 3LR

17 2

Printed in Malaysia

Contents

Flomper and the Flyaway Fairies

Flomper snuggled up in bed and smiled happily as his mum read him a wonderful story. It was all about fairies that had come to visit the meadow in which they lived. The fairies were sprinkling magic dust everywhere, and it made everyone's wishes come true!

"How lovely it would be to see fairies," Flomper said, as his mum finished the story. "How I'd love to fly around with them. Do you think my ears have grown big enough for me to fly with?"

"I don't think so!" laughed his mum. "Ears are for hearing, not flying, Flomper. Rabbits don't fly like fairies can."

Flomper smiled at her. He knew she was wrong. He was sure that his ears would soon help him fly. Just as he was sure he'd see a fairy one day!

"Do you think fairies will come to visit us, Mummy?" he asked her.

"Maybe," she smiled. "If we're lucky."

Flomper felt lucky. He knew he would have such fun with the fairies if they came. "Please, please visit me, fairies!" he wished as he bounded across the field to search for them, gazing up into the sky as he went.

BASH! BOING! Whoops! Flomper was so busy looking into the sky for the fairies that he didn't see the tree until it was too late! He sat back and rubbed his sore nose. He could do with some magical fairy dust right now to make it better!

Next, Flomper looked under bushes, behind trees and even down a few rabbit holes. But there was no sign of any fairies anywhere. Finally, he gave up. He was so tired after all his searching that he curled up in his burrow and had a lovely dream… about fairies!

Suddenly Flomper felt something tickle his ear. He twitched it. But it tickled again. And then he heard the prettiest little laugh.

Flomper's eyes shot open. He gasped. It was dark in his burrow but he was sure he'd just

caught sight of something with shimmering wings flying out of the hole. It was a fairy! He was sure of it!

"Stop!" he yelled, bounding out after her. "Don't go! Wait!" He stopped, looking around and blinking in the sunlight.

"What's the matter, darling?" asked his mum, hopping over.

"Didn't you see that fairy?" Flomper cried.

His mum shook her head. "I'm sorry," she said, "but I was behind that bush over there."

Flomper looked desperately all around him. But he couldn't see the fairy anywhere.

"I frightened her," he said miserably. "I yelled so loudly, I scared her away."

"Oh well, I expect she'll come back," said his mum.

Flomper frowned. He wasn't so sure. He'd made such a racket. And then he'd chased after the poor fairy. No wonder she'd been scared. But that was only a few seconds ago. Surely she couldn't have flown far away? Maybe she was still watching him?

"Please come back, fairy!" he whispered.

And then he heard fluttering nearby.

Flomper and the Flyaway Fairies

Flomper held his breath and turned his head very, very slowly. But it was only leaves falling to the floor as Suzie the squirrel bounded along a branch.

"What was all the shouting about?" asked Suzie.

"Yes, tell us!" cried Floss, Flomper's sister, peering out of a hole. "You woke me up!"

"I saw a fairy," said Flomper, excitedly. "Did you?"

"No," said Suzie.

"I was asleep," Floss yawned.

Suzie peered around her. "I can't see her anywhere. I'll go to the top of that tree and have a look for her." But Suzie couldn't see the fairy even from up there.

"She's gone!" wailed Flomper, sadly. "She's flown away and now she'll never come back."

"Perhaps you should fly after her," giggled Floss. "You always say that one day you're going to fly with those big ears of yours."

"Yes!" cried Flomper, excitedly.

"I was joking…" Floss said.

But Flomper wasn't. "I'm going to do it!" he cried and bounded off to the top of the nearest hill. Floss and Suzie rushed after him and watched as Flomper stood there, tingling all over with excitement. He was going to do it! He was going to fly! He just knew it.

"Flomper!" cried his mum, racing after him. "Be careful. Bunnies don't fly…"

Flomper smiled at her. This bunny did. He knew he could fly! He'd always known he'd do it one day. And this was the day. He took a deep breath, held out his ears as wide as he could, ran and then jumped!

"Wheee!" he cried. It was amazing, it was brilliant, it was… ow! Flomper went *Bump! Thump! Bumpity-bump!* as he hit the ground and bounced down the hill.

"Flomper!" called his mum and Floss.

"I'm okay!" cried Flomper from the bramble bush where he had landed. "Ouch!" he whispered as he pulled the prickles out.

"My poor little bunny," said his mum, bounding down to him.

"Oh, you were so funny!" giggled Floss.

"Are you okay?" asked Suzie.

"I'm fine," said Flomper, getting up. "I just need to find another way to fly. Maybe I need some feathers. Can you help me find them?"

"I'm not sure…" began his mum, but Suzie and Floss helped Flomper look for feathers. They then helped stick them in his fur, and with two big peacock feathers in each paw, Flomper took off again while his mum covered her eyes. She was too scared to watch!

"Wheee!" cried Flomper excitedly. This time he flew much further – and landed straight in the bramble bush.

"Dear Flomper, please stop trying to fly," begged his mum, helping him up. "I've told you before that it is ever so dangerous."

"But I have to find the fairy – and fast!" cried Flomper. "I have to tell her that I wasn't cross with her, that I want her to come back. I have to try to fly again."

But how? The little bunny scratched his head. And then, suddenly, he knew!

"Wait here!" he cried and he ran all the way home to their burrow. He had to hunt under coats and blankets and pillows and scarves, but finally he found just what he was looking for. It was old and pink and purple, but it was just perfect!

Clutching it tightly, Flomper ran all the way back up to the others at the top of the hill.

"Can I borrow your umbrella?" he asked his mum, as he put it up.

"Um, I suppose so…" she said. Before she could change her mind, holding it as high as he could, Flomper ran and jumped. As he did, a sudden gust of wind came and took him up into the sky.

"Wheee!" Flomper cried, as the wind whistled through his fur. "I'm flying!" And this time, he really was!

Everyone was staring, shocked! Flomper's mum, Floss, Suzie and all the other animals, insects and birds all around stared in amazement. No one had ever seen a bunny fly before!

And Flomper didn't just fly; he soared above the trees and across the valley, higher and higher. It was brilliant. It was fantastic! It was wonderful!

Bluey the bluebird flew after him, but she could hardly keep up.

"Flomper! Are you all right?" she tweeted, anxiously.

Flomper and the Flyaway Fairies

"Yes!" giggled Flomper. "I'm fine. In fact I'm better than fine. I'm the happiest bunny in the whole wide world."

And then, faintly at first, Flomper heard a wonderful tinkling sound. It was a fairy! No it wasn't, it was three fairies!

As Flomper started to float back down they all joined Bluey in flying around him, keeping him safe.

"I'm sorry!" Flomper said to the fairies, "I never meant to…"

Suddenly there was a huge gust of wind. *Rrrrrrip!* Flomper looked up. Oh no! A big hole had appeared in his mum's umbrella. And he was suddenly going down. Fast!

"Help!" he shrieked as fields and trees and a big lake came rushing up to meet him.

Flomper closed his eyes. He'd really done it now. If his little yell before had scared one fairy away, that big shriek surely had terrified all three of them forever!

And then something strange started happening. He wasn't going down quite as fast as before … and now he was actually going back up again.

He opened his eyes and stared. The three fairies were holding on to him and keeping him up. They were flying with him!

As he gazed at them in wonder, all three fairies giggled their pretty tinkling laughs.

"You've saved me!" whispered Flomper.

"Yes!" said the blue fairy.

"Of course we did," added the pink and green ones.

"Thank you so much!" cried Flomper. "I'm so sorry, I never meant to scare you away. I love fairies. I've always wanted you to visit me. I want to be your friend. My name is Flomper."

"That's good!" laughed the pink fairy. "Because we want to be your friend, too! It's nice to meet you – we are the Flyaway Fairies!"

"Hooray!" Flomper cried, as they all flew through the air together. "So you'll come back again?"

"Every day!" the fairies said. "And this is so much fun that, if it's okay with you, we'd like to take you flying with us every time!"

Flomper couldn't believe his ears. The fairies were his friends. They would be coming back every day – to take him flying! All his wishes had suddenly come true. Not only was he flying through the air, but he was also over the moon!

Vincent's
Second Voice

Vincent was a strange little boy. Whenever there were adults around, he was an absolute angel. He would help elderly people cross the street, he would run errands for his mother whenever she asked, and he would never interrupt while his teacher was teaching.

"My Vincent is such a good little boy," his mother would boast. "He never tells fibs or complains about eating vegetables."

"He is such a delight in the classroom!" his teacher agreed. "He is just so well behaved."

"Oh, Vincent will grow up into a fine young man," the old lady next door would always say.

Now, you might ask, what was so strange about that? Vincent may have seemed too good to be true, but that wasn't so unusual, was it? No, the strange thing was that while adults loved him dearly, children thought Vincent was an absolute terror!

He would push and shove his sister, quarrel with other children, and get others into trouble, while he himself would get away scot-free.

"Vincent broke my doll!" sobbed his little sister, Judy. But their mother thought that Vincent was such a good boy, that she just could not believe that he would do such a thing.

"Vincent never, ever, *ever* does his homework!" said Mary, the smartest girl in his class. "He always copies mine – sometimes, he even steals it!" But the teacher didn't believe her.

"Vincent always cheats at games," said Tom, Vincent's classmate. "And if he is losing, he ruins the game, or just walks away!"

The truth was that Vincent really was two-faced! He always took care to be good when there were grown-ups around, but was absolutely horrid to children.

One day, Vincent was playing hide-and-seek in the woods with the other schoolchildren. It was Vincent's turn to hide. He climbed into the hollow of a large tree.

"This is such a good place!" he chuckled. "Nobody will find me here!"

But what he did not know was that a small

elf was sleeping underneath him! You see, the elf, whose name was Boffin, was on his way to his home in the magic woods, but had stopped for a rest on the way. He had climbed into the hollow so that nobody would find him. Boffin had been snoring away happily, covered in a cosy blanket of leaves, when he suddenly felt a heavy weight on his middle.

"Mmmmf!" Boffin cried. "Get off me!"

Vincent was startled. What was that noise? He climbed back out of the tree and looked inside. He saw the little elf, curled up in the

bottom of the tree hollow. Now, Vincent wasn't very smart. He didn't notice Boffin's pointed ears or the tiny bells on his shoes. He thought that the elf was just a small child. And you know how Vincent behaved with children!

"You little pipsqueak!" Vincent said rudely. "I'm playing hide-and-seek! Be quiet, or I will stamp all over you!" And he climbed back on top of the elf.

Boffin was taken aback. He didn't know what to do! Vincent was already so heavy and so much bigger than he was. He certainly didn't want to get into a fight with him.

A few minutes later, Vincent's friend Luke came towards the tree in which Vincent was hiding. Boffin heard footsteps and tried to yell, but Vincent was sitting right on his tummy and he couldn't catch enough breath to shout out.

"Oh, how I hope he is found!" thought Boffin. "Then I'll be able to breathe again."

After looking in the bushes and up all the trees, Luke spotted the tree with the yawning hollow in its trunk.

"Aha!" he said. "I'll bet someone is hiding in there!"

Vincent's Second Voice

Sure enough, when Luke peeked into the hole, he saw Vincent crouched down inside – and poor Boffin under him!

"Vincent!" he cried, "Come out of there! You're sitting on someone!"

Grumbling loudly, Vincent climbed out of the hollow. Luke peered in. "Are you all right there?" he asked Boffin.

"Oh, I'm fine now!" replied the elf. "Thank you for rescuing me. That wretched boy would never have got off me, otherwise. I need to teach him a lesson!"

But Vincent was nowhere to be seen.

"Oh bother!" said Luke. "That Vincent! I caught him fair and square! Now he's gone off and hidden again."

"Why is he so rude?" asked Boffin. "Everyone must really dislike him!"

"Oh no," said Luke. "Not everyone. Adults absolutely adore Vincent. He is horrid to us children, but a complete angel to them!"

"Oh ho!" said Boffin, stroking his chin. "I must see this for myself! Let's go and find him and see what we can do about it."

Boffin climbed out of the tree hollow, and

snapped his fingers three times. All at once, he shot up by three feet! His clothes transformed into a coat and trousers, and his cap into a woolly hat that covered his ears.

"Why, you look just like an old man now!" said Luke.

"Ha, ha, ha!" laughed Boffin. "Let's see how Vincent treats me now!"

The elf had very sharp eyes. He spotted Vincent climbing a tree in the distance. He and Luke ran towards the tree, shouting up at him as they got nearer.

"Come out, Vincent!" said Luke, looking up the tree. "I've found you!"

"No you haven't!" retorted Vincent. "Climb up and catch me, slowcoach!"

"That's cheating, Vincent," said Luke. "I only have to spot you. I don't have to catch you." Then, in a loud voice, he added, "Don't you think so, sir?"

At that moment, much to Vincent's shock, Boffin walked up to the tree, frowning up at him.

"Oh yes," he said to Luke. "It is cheating, indeed – what an awfully naughty thing to do!"

Vincent's Second Voice

Vincent clambered down the tree as fast as he could. He didn't want an adult to see how badly he was behaving.

"Oh, I was just joking," he said. Then he turned to Boffin with a charming smile. "Sir, do you need some help? Are you lost?"

"Yes, I am!" replied Boffin. "Would you be so kind as to show me the way back to town?"

"Of course, sir!" said Vincent. "Why, I'll take you there myself! I can play with my friends another day."

"There's really no need for that," said Boffin. "But thank you for offering. You certainly are a polite child." And off he went in the direction that Vincent had indicated. But instead of walking away, Boffin hid behind a tree to see what Vincent would do next.

No sooner had he gone out of sight, than Vincent's smile turned into a nasty scowl. "Silly old man!" he said. "Surely even an old fool like him can find the way back to town!"

Then he rounded on Luke and grabbed him by the arm. "Right, Luke. You're my prisoner now. I caught you fair and square."

Boffin was shocked to see this. He decided

he simply must do something about this horrid child. Suddenly, he had a brilliant idea.

"If Vincent has two faces, I'll give him two voices, too!" he thought. "Then everyone will know what he really thinks of them."

The next day, Vincent woke up early in the morning to go to school. "Good morning, Mummy," he said, with a big yawn.

"Good morning, darling," replied his mother. "Will you go to the shop for me after school? I'm baking a cake for Judy's birthday tomorrow and I need some things."

"Of course, Mummy," he said.

But then, a few seconds later, he spoke again. "I'd rather play with my friends than do your silly grocery shopping, though. Besides, Judy is no fun!"

Vincent was as shocked as his mother. He had never in his life been so rude to her, and he didn't know how he had come to say such a thing out loud.

"I–I didn't say that!" said Vincent, going bright red. "I really didn't. I promise!"

His mother was more shocked than angry.

"Oh, *Vincent*!" she exclaimed. "You must

Vincent's Second Voice

never speak to me like that again!"

"I'm sorry, Mummy," he said. But then a voice added: "No, actually, I'm not!"

Vincent was dumbfounded. He could not understand what was going on. The voice was his and it seemed to be coming from his body, but his lips weren't moving! And now his mother was cross with him. Feeling quite glum, he got ready and went to school.

"Vincent," said his teacher. "Would you please fetch me the green folders from the cupboard?"

"Yes, Miss Brown," said Vincent. But then, the mysterious voice came from nowhere again. "But if you weren't so lazy, you would go and fetch your things for yourself!"

Vincent's hands flew to his mouth. "I did not say that, Miss Brown!"

"Vincent! This is so unlike you," said the teacher. "Are you feeling all right?"

Vincent nodded vigorously, afraid to say anything. Where was this voice coming from?

All day long, Vincent said as little as he could. He did not want to get into any more trouble. After school, Vincent went to the local shop to get the eggs, sugar, butter and milk for Judy's birthday cake. He took the shopping basket up to the counter to pay.

"How are you, Vincent?" he asked, as Vincent often went there to shop for his mother.

"Fine, thank you," said Vincent. "And how are you, sir?"

"Well," the man began with a sigh, "my wife hurt her arm last night, poor thing. She's resting now, but my daughter's getting married soon, so she's still rather busy writing invitations and…"

"How boring!" said the mysterious voice. "Could you just please hurry up, so that I can go and play?"

The man went red with anger, and Vincent was helpless. It was unmistakeably his voice!

"I'm sorry about that, sir," said Vincent, realising that nobody would believe that it wasn't him speaking. "I don't know what's got into me today. I feel rather ill. I think I should go home."

Vincent left the still fuming shopkeeper and rushed home. He didn't stop to chat with anyone. He went straight to his room and shut the door. He flopped down on his bed in despair. What on earth was going on?

"Who are you?" he demanded out loud. "And why are you using my voice to say mean things?"

To Vincent's great surprise, he actually received an answer. "I'm your second voice, Vincent," it said. "And I am only saying the things that you are thinking!"

"What nonsense!" said Vincent, angrily. "Nobody has two voices!"

"Nobody should be two-faced either, Vincent," replied the voice. "But you are. You have one face for adults, and another for children. If you want to get rid of your second voice, you must also get rid of your second face!" Actually, the second voice was Boffin's, who had made himself invisible and was speaking in Vincent's voice, throwing it as if it came from Vincent.

"Oh dear," said Vincent, his forehead furrowing with worry. "What am I going to do now?" He truly believed that he now had a second voice. He had no way of knowing that

Boffin was doing this to him.

"It's not that hard!" said the second voice. "You have to treat everyone with respect. Don't talk behind people's backs, and be kind to everyone."

Vincent thought about what his second voice had said. Whilst he had this second voice, it didn't seem as though he had any option. "This is going to be very hard work for me," he thought. But it was certainly worth a try.

Before he dared to speak to any adults, he decided that he would first try talking to his sister. He opened the door to his bedroom and called out, "Hey, Judy! Come on, let's go and play!"

At first, little Judy was rather puzzled, as Vincent was usually so mean and nasty. But he seemed to be keen to join in with her game, and she was delighted that her brother wanted to play. "Let's have a tea party!" she said. "Come, I will introduce you to my guests. Here's Miss Anne, that is Mr Theodore, and those are the Johnson twins…"

Judy introduced Vincent to all her little toys. Then she gave him a tiny cup and saucer.

Vincent's Second Voice

Although he thought that playing with Judy would be boring, Vincent could see that Judy was very happy. And all because he had agreed to play with her!

"This is delicious, Judy," said Vincent, as he sipped on his imaginary tea. This was obviously a lie, and he expected his second voice to speak up. But it didn't!

"That was surprisingly easy – and sort of fun, too!" thought Vincent, perking up a little. "I think I'll go to the playground and practise being nice to someone else."

Carrying his football, Vincent made his way to the playground. His friends were already playing. "Hi, can I join in?" called Vincent.

"We're already in the middle of a game," said one of the boys. "You'll have to wait."

Vincent went red in the face. He had walked all the way to the playground, and his friends were refusing to let him play!

"You are all so unkind to me! You never let me play with you!" shouted Vincent. "I'll just go and play with my other friends!"

Then his second voice spoke up again! "I'm sorry," he heard himself saying. "I'm just

mean and spoiled, and I can't bear it when I don't get my own way! I don't even have any other friends. Please let me play."

The boys all began to laugh at him.

"Ha, ha! That's true enough!" said Luke, in between bouts of laughter. "Go and throw your tantrums somewhere else." Vincent didn't know where to look! He ran back home, almost in tears, and dashed up to his room.

"Oh, you terrible, terrible voice!" he said. "I really don't like you!"

"Just as nobody likes your two faces!" said the voice.

At that moment, Boffin jumped down from the top of the wardrobe. "Hello, Vincent. Do you remember me?"

"What are you doing here?" asked a startled Vincent. "You're the funny-looking boy from the tree hollow!"

"I am also the old man you offered to take to the town!" said Boffin. "Remember him?"

"That was you?" Vincent asked, taken aback and quite puzzled.

"I wanted to teach you a lesson," said Boffin. "I've seen how you are only polite to adults so that you can get away with your bullying ways with other children."

Vincent's lower lip trembled, as if he was about to burst into tears. "That's not true!" he said.

"That is very true," said Boffin. But although he had wanted to teach Vincent a lesson, he hadn't wished to upset him dreadfully. Fortunately, Boffin was a kind-hearted elf.

"Don't worry," he said gently. "It's easy to drive away your second voice. Do you want to know the secret?"

"Yes," said Vincent. "Yes! I'll do anything!"

"All you have to do is learn to be good to everyone around you – adults *and* children," replied Boffin.

"But what if they annoy me?" asked Vincent. "Or if they are mean to me?"

"Could it be that they are only that way because of the way you treat them?" suggested Boffin. "Perhaps if you are kinder to them, they will behave differently towards you."

"I promise I will try," said Vincent.

That night, he began making a birthday

present for Judy. By bedtime, Vincent could hardly keep his eyes open. It had been a very long day!

In the morning, the first thing he did was to go to Judy's room. He was sure that she would like the present he had made her.

"Happy birthday, Judy!" he said, giving her the present. When Judy unwrapped the wrapping paper, she was delighted. It was a wooden pencil box that Vincent had made from ice-cream sticks.

"Thank you!" she said, clutching the pencil box to her chest.

"How are you feeling today, Vincent?" asked his mother.

"I'm all right now, I think," said Vincent. "I'm sorry about my awful behaviour yesterday."

Vincent apologised to his teacher and the man at the corner store, too. They were all glad to see that his rude outbursts had stopped, and that he was being polite again – only this time, he was sincere; he wasn't two-faced any more! The real test was going to be how he behaved with the other children.

Popular Rewards

That afternoon after school, Vincent went to the playground, where the rest of the class were playing football. "I am sorry for being mean to all of you," he said. "I promise I'll be nice from now on. Now, how about a game of football? I'll wait if you have already started playing."

Needless to say, his friends were quite shocked! "Why, Vincent," said his friend, Pat. "This is quite a change from your usual self. I wonder how long it'll last."

At these words, Vincent felt a flood of anger rushing through him. But then he remembered what Boffin had told him. He calmed down immediately.

"I will try to make it last as long as I can," he said in earnest.

Luke walked up to Vincent and put his arm around his shoulder.

"Come on then, Vincent!" he said. "I can tell that you've really changed. Let's have that game of football!"

And even though his team lost, Vincent played until the very end of the game. It was so much fun! "I always thought football was

all about winning," he thought, "but now I understand that it's just a fun game!"

Vincent's friends wanted him to stay for another game, but he explained that he had to go home.

"It would be great to stay and keep playing," he told them. "But it's my sister's birthday, and she'll be upset if I'm not there for her party."

Boffin was watching Vincent from a corner of the playground.

"So, he's learnt to put others before himself," said the elf. "Excellent!"

At the birthday party, Vincent was a kind host, even though there were no other children of his age there. He helped his father blow up the balloons and his mother serve the cake. He even told funny stories to all of Judy's young friends!

"You have such a nice brother!" they told her. Judy was very proud to hear that. She had a wonderful birthday party!

That night, while Vincent was getting ready for bed, Boffin appeared again in his room.

"Hello, Vincent," said the elf. "Have you had a good day?"

"It was amazing!" said Vincent. "My second voice didn't make a sound all day."

"Well," said Boffin. "That means that you haven't been two-faced today! Was it really difficult?"

"A little," said Vincent, "but it will get easier."

Boffin gave him a big grin. "Well then, my job here is done," he said. "I'll see you around, Vincent. Toodle pip!" And with a *pop*, Boffin disappeared.

Vincent was right. It *did* get easier for him to stop being two-faced. Soon, he was as popular with children as he was with adults. And no one called him Two-Faced Vincent ever again!

Candytuft's Butterflies

The residents of Skillston were very, very talented. Everyone was good at something or other. Candytuft was a little brownie who lived in Skillston. His father was very good at pie-eating contests and his mother had a patch of prize-winning pumpkins in their back garden.

As for little Candytuft, he did not yet know what his skill was, and he was running out of time. By the age of eight, all of the residents of Skillston had usually fully developed their talents. But there was no sign of Candytuft's talent, even though his eighth birthday had been three months ago. What's more, all the eight-year-old children of Skillston had to show their skills to the entire town at the yearly talent show, which was taking place the following weekend. Candytuft was in trouble!

"Don't worry, Candytuft," said his mother.

"If nothing else works, you can always pretend to pull your thumb off... oh, or maybe you could produce a coin from behind someone's ear?"

"No!" wailed Candytuft. "Those are just simple tricks. I want to find my *real* skill."

For the next week, Candytuft tried everything he possibly could. He tried to hula-hoop, but he had no rhythm and couldn't keep it spinning. Next, he tried to balance a ball on the tip of his nose, but his neck began to ache

terribly. In the end, he even tried producing a coin from behind a little fairy's ear. But she was not impressed in the least! She snatched the coin away and skipped off without so much as a 'thank you'.

"Well, I'm worn out," said Candytuft, sadly. "I still don't have a clue what I'm good at and the talent show is only two days away!"

At bedtime, Candytuft just couldn't get to sleep. He tossed and turned all night. In the morning, he felt more tired than ever.

"I've made your favourite, Candytuft – scrambled eggs," said his mother. "Come down for breakfast, won't you?"

Normally, Candytuft would have come bounding down the stairs for breakfast. But he didn't feel quite right this morning. He held his stomach and rolled around in bed.

"Oh, Mummy," cried Candytuft. "I have the collywobbles! Scrambled eggs won't do. I need some syrup to soothe my tummy."

"Poor dear!" said Candytuft's mother. "Perhaps you're worried about the talent contest. Just relax and calm down. You'll be all right!"

Candytuft tried not to worry about the talent contest. "Everything's going to be fine," he told himself. But the tummy ache refused to go away, even when his mother gave him a spoonful of syrup.

Candytuft decided to visit his friend, Tally-Ho. Tally-Ho's talent was that he was very, very clever. He had already turned nine, so he didn't have to perform in the talent show the next day. When Tally-Ho heard Candytuft's story, he stroked his chin thoughtfully.

"I think I may have something to help you," said Tally-Ho, rummaging through his cupboard. He brought out a little bottle of red liquid and handed it to Candytuft. "This potion should be able to show us what's wrong with your tummy, and help you get rid of it. Give it a try."

Candytuft swallowed every last drop of it, even though it tasted horrid. But he didn't feel better. If anything, he felt even worse.

"Nothing – *hic* – seems to be working," moaned Candytuft. "My tummy – *hic* – feels so tickly! And now I have the hiccups – *HIC*!" Candytuft let out a loud hiccup. As he hiccupped, a little butterfly escaped from his mouth and landed on his nose.

"I knew it!" Tally-Ho exclaimed, snapping his fingers. "You have a case of butterflies in your tummy!"

"Butterflies?" asked Candytuft. "I thought that was just a saying. Surely there can't be butterflies in my stomach?"

"Didn't you just see one pop out?" said Tally-Ho.

"I suppose I did! Well, can you give me some more of that red stuff?" asked Candytuft. "I absolutely have to hiccup all the butterflies out before the talent show tomorrow!"

"It takes me a week to brew the potion, and you've drunk it all," said Tally-Ho. "Let's find another way to get them out."

First, they tried to cough the butterflies out. Candytuft coughed and gasped while Tally-Ho thumped him hard on the back. They thought that maybe Candytuft could sneeze the butterflies out, but it was very hard for him to make himself sneeze and he didn't manage to produce a single butterfly.

"It's no use!" cried Candytuft, holding his

stomach. "I'll make a fool of myself tomorrow, all because of these beastly butterflies!"

"Don't worry, we'll think of something!" said Tally-Ho. "I have a plan. Instead of forcing the butterflies out, why don't we give them a reason to come out themselves? Just think about it – what do butterflies like most?"

Candytuft thought for a moment. "Flowers?" he asked.

"Yes!" said Tally-Ho. "Let's lead them to the most sweet-smelling flowers we can find. That'll draw them right out."

Fortunately, Candytuft's mother didn't grow only prize-winning pumpkins in their back garden; she also grew a great variety of flowers. Candytuft rushed home and stood in the middle of a bed of brilliant red roses. He opened his mouth wide and waited for the butterflies to pop out.

For a while, nothing happened. Then Candytuft began to feel the fluttering in his tummy move slowly upwards. It crept up his chest and into his throat. It filled his mouth and out came a swarm of beautiful butterflies! There were pink ones and blue ones, large ones and tiny ones, all fluttering around Candytuft.

"Oh, my word!" said Tally-Ho, his eyes full of wonder. "I don't think I've ever seen such a delightful sight."

"Good riddance!" said Candytuft, who was not at all amused. "And right on time, too – Mummy will serve supper any minute now. Then it's straight to bed for me. Tomorrow is the talent show and I must be fresh for that." He still didn't know what he was going to do at the talent show, but he was hopeful that something would come to mind.

Candytuft ate his supper and quickly went to bed. Soon, he was fast asleep. He truly was very, very tired. In the morning, his mother shook him awake.

"Wake up, Candytuft," she called. "It's time for breakfast. I've made another of your favourites – buttered crumpets. Come on now. Today is the talent show!"

Candytuft groaned. He did not want to be reminded of the contest. At breakfast, Candytuft ate all of the crumpets, one after the other.

"Now that the butterflies have gone, I might

have some time to practise," he thought. "I'll pretend to pull off my thumb so well that everyone will believe me."

Candytuft practised hard all morning. Soon, it was time for him to leave for the competition. "I may not have a real talent," he thought, "but at least there are no butterflies in my tummy. I'm sure that at least my parents and Tally-Ho will cheer for me."

At the venue, all the other eight-year-olds of Skillston were waiting backstage for their turn to perform. When they saw Candytuft, they all began to giggle.

"What's your talent?" one young brownie teased. "I heard that you don't have one!"

Candytuft went red with anger. "I do!" he said. "Just you wait and see!"

"I bet it's something silly, like pretending to pull off your thumb," scoffed another brownie.

Candytuft's cheeks turned bright pink. Suddenly, he didn't feel very confident any more. He began to sweat and the fluttering in his tummy started once again. But it was too late to do anything – the talent show had begun. The pixies, gnomes and elves all went up on stage, one by one.

"Oh no," Candytuft cried. "The butterflies are back!" It was unmistakeable. He could even feel their little wings flapping around in his tummy. Just then, his name was called. It was time for him to go on stage.

The little brownie quaked with fear as he walked on stage. Through the blinding spotlights, he could see his mother and father in the crowd, full of pride.

Next to them was Tally-Ho, who gave him two thumbs up. Candytuft did not want to let them down.

He cleared his throat and held out his hands in front of him. But just as he was about to begin his act, he felt a sharp pain in his stomach. "Ow!" he yelled, in front of the entire audience.

Candytuft blushed. "I'm sorry," he said. "But I seem to have a terrible case of butterflies in my tummy!"

The crowd laughed. They thought Candytuft just meant that he was very nervous. Only Tally-Ho understood what he meant. He immediately sprang up from his seat and rushed backstage to help his friend.

Tally-Ho wasn't known as the smartest brownie in Skillston without good reason. He immediately rushed to the table where the winners' prizes were kept. On it was a bouquet of beautiful flowers. Tally-Ho grabbed the flowers before anyone could stop him. He ran out to the front and threw the bouquet into Candytuft's hands.

Before Candytuft could work out what was happening, he felt the fluttering move up his chest, through his throat and out of his mouth. The butterflies swirled and danced around him, while the audience gasped in surprise.

By the time the butterflies had all come out, the people in the audience had stood up to give

him an incredibly loud round of applause.

"What a splendid talent!" they exclaimed to one another. "I have never seen anything quite like it!"

Candytuft took a bow and hurried off stage, the butterflies pursuing him. "Get rid of the bouquet!" suggested Tally-Ho, as he walked up and gave Candytuft an encouraging pat on the shoulder. As soon as Candytuft threw the bouquet away, the butterflies flitted away after it.

"Phew!" said Candytuft. "Those butterflies just wouldn't leave me alone. I don't think I want to see another butterfly ever again!"

"They *did* help you to do really well in the talent show, though, didn't they?" said Tally-Ho. "Maybe that is your real talent!"

Just then, they heard the host announcing, "The results are in. The winner of the talent show is... Candytuft!"

Candytuft couldn't believe his ears. Tally-Ho had to push him back onto the stage to accept his prize! He watched proudly as the host pinned a ribbon to his best friend's chest and handed him *another* bouquet of flowers.

Candytuft's Butterflies

And, as Candytuft accepted the bouquet, he hiccupped, letting out another butterfly. Isn't that a funny talent to have?

The Cottage Ghost

Ted and his wife, Mabel, were a kindly old couple who lived in the city with their dog, Angus. The three of them were very happy together. But, as is usually the case with the elderly, Ted and Mabel's senses were getting weaker. Ted couldn't hear very well and Mabel was extremely short-sighted, yet they both still had a very good sense of humour.

"Have you fed the dog, dear?" Mabel would ask.

"No, I haven't wed a frog," replied Ted. "I married you, didn't I?"

Mabel could be quite silly herself! Once, they were both in a rush to get ready for a wedding. "Mabel, dear," called Ted. "I can't for the life of me find my polka dot bow tie!"

"Pah!" said Mabel, raising her arms in frustration. "You're the one with the good eyes, and yet you make me do these things..." Mabel walked over to the wardrobe. She

The Cottage Ghost

glanced into the part where Ted kept all his bow ties, put her hand in, and brought out the polka dot one with no effort at all. Even though her eyesight wasn't very good, Mabel's memory was still very sharp.

"Here it is," she said, triumphantly. "Now I expect you'll want me to put it on you, too." She walked over to her husband and began adjusting the bow tie around his neck.

"How is it that I manage to find your things, when you can't? What would you do without me, Ted? Ted? Ted – why aren't you answering me?"

Ted wasn't answering her because he was too busy laughing. She wasn't putting the bow tie on him, but on the coat stand!

Ted and Mabel loved each other very much. Even with all their mishaps, they managed quite well for themselves. They always supported each other and, of course, they had Angus to help them and protect them from thieves and tricksters.

One day, the old couple were relaxing in their living room. Ted was reading the newspaper in his armchair, while Mabel was sitting in her rocking chair, knitting a tea cosy.

"Ted, dear," said Mabel. "Why don't we sell the house and live in the country?"

"You're barmy!" replied Ted. "Why would I want to smell a mouse and live in the pantry?"

"That's not what I said, dear," said Mabel. "I said that we should shift homes."

"I don't want to gift combs to anybody, Mabel," said Ted. "Most of my friends are completely bald. Anyway, I've had an idea – why don't we sell this place and buy a nice country home?"

Mabel just smiled in the general direction of her husband. Though her husband couldn't hear her very well, he somehow always managed to get her message. And though

The Cottage Ghost

Mabel could no longer see her husband's face clearly, she certainly thought he was still the most handsome man in the world.

Soon, Ted and Mabel found someone to buy their city home, and bought a lovely old cottage in the countryside. It was an old house, but, with some work, they were able to make it look nice.

Their countryside cottage was a pretty blue colour with a white roof. It had a large garden with lots of flowers and birds. But the very best thing about their new home was that their back gate opened straight onto the seashore.

"It's all so pretty," sighed Mabel.

"No, it's not the city," said Ted, "but I wouldn't worry. It's a hundred times lovelier here. And this home is delightful! It's a wonder that we got it so cheaply."

"Woof!" barked Angus, in agreement. He immediately went off to explore the area.

But the three of them didn't know that their cottage was already occupied by a strange kind of lodger. It was a ghost that had been there for several years, and was in no mood to leave!

That afternoon, Mabel was preparing tea

in the kitchen when the ghost floated through the wall and appeared next to her.

"You look awfully pale, Ted," said Mabel, squinting at the ghost. "Some fresh air would do you good. Shall we have a picnic on the seashore?"

"Aaaaaargh!" the ghost screamed frightfully. He wanted to give Mabel a good scare. But instead of being frightened, Mabel was only concerned. "Oh my!" she said. "Are you in pain? Should I call an ambulance?"

Gesturing towards the kitchen chair, she instructed the ghost to sit down. She rushed into the living room, where they kept the telephone. Ted was sitting in the armchair, reading the newspaper.

"Ted?" asked Mabel, squinting. "Is that you? Then who is in the kitchen?"

"You want me to get you a pigeon?" asked Ted, scratching his head. "Well, all right, then..." But before he could say any more, Mabel grabbed his arm and pulled him into the kitchen, where the ghost was still floating around.

"Hallo!" said Ted, waving cheerily at the

The Cottage Ghost

frightful figure. "Why, you look as pale as a ghost! Join us for a spot of tea – I insist."

"Silence!" yelled the ghost. "I *am* a ghost!"

"Now, now, Mister," said Ted wearily. "You most certainly are *not* the host. *We* are the hosts."

"No, no, Ted," explained Mabel. "He says that he's a ghost – you know, like a phantom… I would have been afraid, but all I could see was a very pale, blurry person."

"Oh, don't call our friend a furry bison," said Ted. "That's rather rude, and not very accurate at all. I'd say he looks more like a polar bear..."

The ghost was furious. It began whizzing around the kitchen, contorting its face into horrible expressions while producing all sorts of frightening sounds. But all its efforts were lost on Mabel and Ted.

"Ha, ha, ha!" laughed Ted, pointing at the ghost. "You can pull some really funny faces, can't you? And look at how you move! I daresay you're throwing a tantrum because I called you a polar bear. It was only a joke! Why don't you calm down and have some tea?"

Meanwhile, Mabel could only hear the ghost's screeches and wails. "I can't tell whether you're laughing or crying," she told the ghost. "Why can't we all just sit down and talk like adults?"

Just then, Angus came bounding into the house, tired after a long day of chasing seagulls and sniffing flowers. Seeing the ghost, he began to bark loudly. Angus was not a very large dog, but having lived with Ted and Mabel for a few years, he had learnt how to make his presence felt. He ran around the ghost,

The Cottage Ghost

barking loudly, drowning out the sounds of the ghost's cries.

Feeling very frustrated, the ghost let out one last blood-curling scream and shot up through the chimney, never to be seen again.

"Why did he use the chimney?" wondered Ted. "We have a perfectly good door."

"Never mind that, Ted," said Mabel. "Let's have some tea. I've made some scones that we can have with strawberry jam and clotted cream. I have an idea – why don't we pack it all up and have a picnic on the beach?"

"A pig kicked in the teeth?" asked Ted. "I've got to see this! Did it happen on the beach? Let's go at once!"

Walking arm-in-arm, as they always did (they had to, or Mabel would completely lose her way), they made their way to the beach through the back gate, with Angus following eagerly behind.

Ted, Mabel and Angus lived happily in their cottage for many years, and they enjoyed many more picnics by the seaside. But not once did that ghost – or any other ghost – bother them ever again.

Camp Astoria

The fairy kingdom of Finkleton was celebrating. The fairy queen had given birth to a beautiful baby girl. She had large blue eyes, which is why her parents called her Azura, or Azzy for short.

Azzy grew up into a lovely little girl. She was graceful, polite and loved to read books.

But since there were no other fairy children of her age in the kingdom, Azzy did not have any friends. The king and queen were getting quite worried about their daughter. One day, they sat her down for a talk.

"Azzy, dear," said the king. "Wouldn't you like some children of your own age to play with?"

"Not really," said Azzy with a shrug.

"But, my love," said the queen, "it would do you a lot of good. That is why we have enrolled you into Camp Astoria. It's a camp especially for fairy princesses, just like you!"

Azzy frowned, thinking to herself: "I don't want to go. What if the other princesses don't like me?"

Seeing the glum look on her face, the king smiled. "I am sure you'll do just fine, dear," he said.

On the day she was to leave for camp, Azzy kissed her mother and father goodbye and climbed onto the back of an enchanted bluebird. Azzy waved to them as the bird spread its wings and they began the long journey to Camp Astoria. They soared high above the vast kingdom of Finkleton, over waterfalls, emerald forests and purple snow-capped mountains before descending towards a stretch of beautiful meadowland, dotted with colourful flowers.

Azzy began to feel nervous again, but she knew she had to be brave.

"Thank you, bird," said Azzy, sweetly. "I wish you could stay with me. Please go back to Finkleton and tell Mother and Father that I'm all right."

The bird chirped happily and flew off. As Azzy watched it disappear over the horizon, she felt a tap on her shoulder. When she turned around, she saw a beautiful adult fairy smiling at her warmly.

"Hello there," said the fairy. "I'm Marisol, the guide at Camp Astoria. You must be Princess Azura, from the kingdom of Finkleton."

"I'm happy to meet you, Marisol," said Azzy, curtsying low. "But please, call me Azzy."

"Very well, Princess Azzy," the fairy said. "Allow me to guide you to your room."

Marisol led Azzy towards a sprawling

garden, filled with all different kinds of flowers. There were lots of other young fairy princesses fluttering around the place, whispering excitedly to one another.

"They've already made friends with each other," thought Azzy, with a hollow feeling deep in her tummy. "Why would they want to bother with me?"

"There's your flower, Princess Azzy," said Marisol, pointing towards a yellow tulip. "We'll see you in the evening, once you're fresh and rested."

Azzy rushed into her tulip, eager to rest. But to her great surprise, another fairy was already inside, merrily unpacking her belongings!

"I'm sorry," said Azzy, blushing nervously. "Marisol must have brought me here by mistake."

"Don't be silly," said the fairy. "You're Azura of Finkleton, aren't you? I'm your roommate, Bucky of Wondertilly."

"Hello," said Azzy, quickly turning away. She was not used to talking to other children. It made her quite anxious. She didn't even tell Bucky to call her Azzy, instead of Azura.

Camp Astoria

"Well," said Bucky, "I've finished unpacking, so I'm going outside to talk to the other princesses. It was nice meeting you!"

Azzy was all alone once again. "I had better go outside," she said to herself sternly. "I'm here to make friends, and I should try my best."

Outside, there were groups of little fairies all around, talking and having a good time. Suddenly, Azzy felt less brave about talking to the other fairies. She twirled her hair anxiously. Nobody so much as glanced in her direction.

That evening, they had a bonfire supper. Food was served on large tree stumps. There were toasted nuts and mugs of warm, frothy malted milk. The young fairies sang, danced and joked together.

Azzy enjoyed the singing and dancing, but she still didn't make any friends. The other fairy princesses smiled at her when they made eye contact, but Azura felt very shy about starting a conversation.

"It's time to sleep, princesses," announced Marisol when it started to get dark. "Today was fun, but tomorrow we're going hiking. So get some rest!"

Azzy had no time to feel sorry for herself. She returned to her tulip and fell asleep immediately, tired from her long journey and the excitement of the day. The next morning, she was woken up by a shrill whistling sound.

"Come along, fairy princesses," said Marisol. "Form groups of five. You're going to learn a lot of new things about fairy magic today."

Azzy sprang out of bed, feeling excited. She loved learning about fairy magic, and already knew a thing or two about using it. She got dressed immediately and bounded outside. But when she saw the other girls already in groups of five, her heart sank.

Just then, Azzy felt a tap on her shoulder. It was Bucky. "Hi, Azura! Would you like to join our group?" she asked. "We're a member short!" Azzy nodded eagerly, a smile appearing on her lips.

Bucky led her to a group of three other fairy princesses. They were Tansy of Flowerford, Whimsy of Cottonleigh and Opal of Jewelwick.

Opal was very, very pretty. She had long,

flaxen hair and a dimpled smile. All the other fairy princesses admired her beauty, especially Tansy and Whimsy. They did whatever she told them to. Bucky already knew Opal as they were from neighbouring kingdoms.

The four girls were pleasant enough to Azzy, but they did not include her in their giggling and chatter as they hiked through the forest. Azzy did not mind. She was much too interested in listening to what Marisol was saying. She was pointing at a big cluster of mushrooms that were growing on the side of a huge tree.

"This is a specimen of *rabidus bisporus*," she said. "Commonly known as..."

"Rabid mushrooms," completed Azzy. "They're called that because of how they latch onto a tree and spread all over it in a matter of hours. In fairy magic, they are commonly used to make luminescence potions."

"Very good, Princess Azura!" said Marisol, looking impressed. "I'm surprised that you even know the word 'luminescence'! You certainly are clever." The other fairies stared at Azura in admiration.

After walking and studying all day, the group came across a waterfall. This was no ordinary waterfall – the water sparkled and shimmered like diamonds.

"This is a magic waterfall," explained Marisol. "It contains some of the best magic water you can use to make potions. You can bathe in the water for a while – I'll be waiting for you here."

"Come on, girls," said Opal. "Let's dive in!" Tansy, Whimsy and Bucky did not need an invitation. They followed Opal eagerly. Azzy, on the other hand, began to rummage in her bag.

"The water is lovely, Azura!" called Bucky. "Won't you join us?"

"In a moment," said Azzy, taking out a large water bottle. She wanted to collect as much magic water as she could, so that she could try making her own magic potions.

Once she had filled the bottle, she replaced the stopper and joined the others for a swim. "This is splendid!" she said to Opal, trying to make conversation.

"I'm bored now," replied Opal, tossing her

Camp Astoria

beautiful hair. "I vote that we explore higher up. I want to see the river that runs into this waterfall."

"Yes, let's!" agreed Tansy and Whimsy, without so much as a second thought.

"I'm not sure we should go off on our own," said Bucky. "We might not be able to find our way back."

"Nonsense," said Opal, "We'll be all right. Marisol won't even realise we've gone."

Bucky shrugged. She didn't agree with Opal, but she did not want to defy her, either. "Are you coming, Azura?" she asked.

"Oh, yes," chimed in Opal. "You should come along, too. We'll have a good time."

Azzy did not know what to do! On the one hand, she absolutely did not want to get into any trouble. On the other hand, this was her chance to make some friends at last!

"Okay, I'll come," she said finally. "We can go this way – it seems like a gentle climb up the mountain and will probably lead us to the river."

"No," said Opal. "Let's go through these bushes. It looks like a much shorter route."

Before Azzy could say anything, Opal had already set off. Tansy, Whimsy and Bucky followed suit. She had no option but to pick up her bag and run to catch up with them.

At first, Azzy felt happy to be included with the others. Bucky was very entertaining. She was quick-witted, funny and very sharp-tongued. Opal told them all about her exciting life in Jewelwick. Tansy and Whimsy were the only ones who didn't have a lot to say – they were much too busy agreeing with Opal on everything she said!

After walking for a while, Azzy realised that she could no longer see the waterfall. She had no idea where they were – and neither did any of the others.

"We've been walking for at least half an hour now," said Bucky. "We ought to have reached the river if we were going in the right direction."

"Let's head back to the waterfall, then," said Opal.

The girls walked and walked, but the waterfall was nowhere to be found. The sun had long since started setting and the crickets had begun to chirp.

"It's getting dark now," said Tansy in a quiet voice. "I'm afraid."

"Me, too," said Whimsy, her voice quivering. "I wish we hadn't wandered off."

"Don't worry," said Azzy. "I think I know how we can get back. You see, this is a tree with the rabid mushrooms that Marisol told us about."

"I don't remember hearing about rabid mushrooms at all," said Opal.

"We're glad *you* paid attention, Azura," said Bucky.

"Yes, very glad," agreed Tansy and Whimsy.

But Azzy was not listening to them. She was thinking up a plan to help them find their way back.

"You look miles away," said Bucky, waving her fingers in front of Azzy's face. "What are you thinking?"

"Rabid mushrooms," explained Azura, "are used to make luminescence potions."

"What is a looming presence?" asked Tansy.

"Lumin*escence* is the shining of a bright light," explained Azura. "What it means is that

I think I can make us glow! I'm sure Marisol and the other guides are looking for us. If we were glowing, it would make it that much easier for them to find us."

"It's a better plan than roaming around in the dark," agreed Opal, grumpily. "Why don't you try it, Azura?"

Azzy opened up her bag and brought out the magic water she had collected from the waterfall. She scraped some of the rabid mushrooms off the tree and mixed them into the water. She added a sprig of ivy and a number of other herbs and plants from the forest floor until she was holding a green potion.

"It's ready," she said finally. "I'll take the first sip." Azzy sipped the potion cautiously.

Slowly, her body began to light up, bit by bit, until she was glowing all over.

The others each took a sip of the potion and soon they were casting enough light to see around themselves clearly as the sun had gone down and it was very dark. They managed to walk a little way without falling over anything.

Suddenly, they heard an agitated voice in the distance. "There you are!" It was Marisol. Her face was as white as a sheet. "You had us all very worried!"

"We are very sorry," said Azzy, when Marisol had made her way over to them. "It won't happen ever again."

"Of course it won't," scolded Marisol. "I am going to send you straight back home for breaking the rules! I waited and waited for you all by the waterfall! Can you imagine what would have happened if five fairy princesses went missing?"

Marisol was very angry with the fairies. Once they were back at the camp, she heard the full story of how Azzy had made the potion. The girls begged and begged not to be sent home. After a while, Marisol softened.

Camp Astoria

"Oh, all right. I will let you girls stay," she said. "But I'm certainly reporting this to your parents. But the letter going to Finkleton will also tell the king and queen how their little daughter brewed a potion and saved her friends."

Soon, everyone at Camp Astoria had heard how Azzy had saved the day. They all wanted to be friends with her. The next morning, several fairy princesses knocked at her tulip. "Come out and play with us, Azura!" they said.

"Call me Azzy!" replied Azzy, before rushing off to play with them.

Inky the
Black Cat

Marla was a beautiful pearl-grey tabby cat with long fluffy fur and green eyes. She lived with the Sedgwick family in a pretty little house. One day, Marla gave birth to a litter of four playful kittens. But none of her kittens looked much like her when they were born! They were skinny things, with bent ears and hardly any fur.

But as the days went by, the kittens grew stronger and braver. Their eyes opened up

and their ears began to stand upright. The Sedgwicks were delighted with the little kittens.

"Well, we can't keep them for long," said Mr Sedgwick, "but we might as well name them while they are with us."

He named the first kitten himself. It was a beautiful white kitten with grey bands across its back. "Why, this little guy is very strong indeed!" exclaimed Daddy Sedgwick. "I'll call him Hercules."

The second kitten was named by Mrs Sedgwick. It was an orange kitten with white paws. "Her name will be Fleur," said Mrs Sedgwick. "It's just as pretty as she is."

"This one is Dash!" said little Reece, pointing to a black-and-white spotted kitten running around his siblings. "He runs so fast!"

Finally, there was only one kitten left – and Freya, the youngest Sedgwick, was given the task of naming him. This kitten was very different from the rest of the litter. He was very small and quiet. But what was most striking about this kitten was his jet-black fur.

"Oh, he's as black as ink!" squealed Freya,

happily. "I think I'll call him Inky."

All of the kittens were very happy at first. But they couldn't stay with the Sedgwicks for long. One by one, they were all adopted. All except Inky, that is. Inky stayed with the Sedgwicks for several more days. Nobody seemed to want him.

"Black cats bring bad luck," people would say. "Why should we bring bad luck upon ourselves?"

Inky didn't really want to leave – he enjoyed living with his mother and the Sedgwicks, especially little Freya. They played together all day long and had lots of fun.

But one day, a man with a heavily wrinkled face came to the Sedgwicks' house.

"Hello, Farmer Joe," said Freya's mother. "What brings you here?"

"I've heard that you have kittens for adoption," replied Farmer Joe. "Can I see them?"

"We only have one left," said Freya. "Little Inky here."

"Inky, eh?" said the man, stroking his chin. "He sure is small. Looks like he was probably the runt of the litter. But he's a sprightly little fellow. I'll have him."

Marla licked Inky's little cheek. She was sad to see him go, but also very excited for him. Freya picked him up and hugged him tightly.

"Goodbye, little Inky," she whispered. "Be a good kitten. I hope you make your new owner very, very happy!"

Inky purred in reply. He hoped that what Freya said would come true. He scampered into a little basket and was taken away by Farmer Joe in his car.

"So, you're a black cat!" he said to Inky. "They say that black cats bring bad luck. As for me, I think that's just an old wives' tale. As long as you can catch all the mice in the barn, you'll bring me plenty of good luck!"

Inky purred with delight. It seemed like this man would be a good owner. His mouth watered at the idea of having lots of mice to eat.

When Inky reached Farmer Joe's farm, he was delighted. It was as if all his dreams had come true! He could roam wherever he liked and explore the fields.

Inky caught every mouse he found. Soon, the mice all learnt to stay away from Farmer Joe's farm. "A ferocious black monster lives there," they would say. "It's best we stay away." With all the mice gone, Inky spent his days lounging lazily in the sun. Farmer Joe was thrilled with Inky and would often sit and eat his lunch in the sun with him, tickling his ears and giving him tasty treats to eat. Inky was a good cat. He was having a wonderful time. But sadly, the other farm animals were getting very jealous of him.

"That Inky's getting tooo cocky for his own goood!" said Connie the cow.

"He puts me in a very baaaad mood!" said Sharon the sheep. The horses whinnied, the hens clucked and the pigs oinked in agreement. They all got together to think up a plan to get rid of poor Inky.

That night, it rained heavily at the farm. There were strong gusts of wind, flashes of lightning and loud claps of thunder. The farm animals decided to go through with their plan. The cows stood outside Farmer Joe's cottage and made very loud noises.

"Booo!" they went. "Booo!"

Inside the cottage, Farmer Joe and his wife, Pauline, were eating dinner when the sound reached their ears. "Can you hear that?" asked his wife.

"Hmm," said Farmer Joe, not paying it much attention. "It must be the animals. They must be frightened by the thunder."

"Animals?" said Pauline. "It most certainly is not! Animals don't say 'Boo!' It's a ghost!"

Farmer Joe dropped his spoon with a clatter. "G–g–ghost?" he asked, gulping in fear. "It c–can't be!"

"Booooooo!"

The farmer and his wife jumped at the sound. "Go out there and check for yourself!" insisted Pauline, pushing her husband towards the door.

Shaking with fear, the farmer opened his wooden door just a crack and peered out fearfully. To his surprise, he saw a dark, monstrous figure looming above him, that appeared to be shaking with rage.

"Booooo!" it went. "Booooo!"

Farmer Joe slammed the door shut, bolting

it frantically. "Pauline! Shut the windows!" he called loudly. "There's some kind of horrible creature out there!"

The two of them spent the whole night cowering in their bed, feeling very afraid. Outside, the animals were rolling around with laughter. The 'monster' had only been the silhouette of a hen standing on a pig, which was standing on a sheep, which was standing on the back of one of the horses!

That wasn't the end of the animals' wicked plan. They crept to the corner of the barn, where Inky was sleeping peacefully. Picking him up by the scruff of his neck, they took him to Farmer Joe's doorstep and left him there.

Now, Inky was a very deep sleeper. He slept through rain, strong winds, lightning and thunder, the cows' deafening noise, and even through being picked up and left on the farmer's doorstep!

He only woke up when he felt a sharp kick on his side. "Out with you!" the farmer's wife yelled. "I knew that black cats were no good! And this one is *very* unlucky! Out!"

Poor Inky didn't know what was happening.

He looked up at Farmer Joe, who was trying to calm Pauline down, but she wouldn't listen. Inky looked around at the farm animals to see if they would help him. But they were just sniggering unpleasantly at him!

Inky knew what he had to do. With a heavy heart, he licked Farmer Joe's hand one last time before running away from the farm. He ran and ran until his paws were sore. Soon, he found himself in a forest and was very tired.

"I'm lost," he thought to himself. "I don't know anybody in this forest! What am I going to do? The animals here are much bigger than I am..." Troubled by his thoughts, Inky curled up into a tiny ball and fell asleep inside a bush.

A few hours later, little Inky woke up with a start. He opened his eyes and saw a face peering back at him: two big eyes, long black hair and a red, smiling mouth. The kitten sat bolt upright in a flash.

"Oh, don't be afraid, little one," croaked the young woman. "I was just picking up some leaves for a potion when I spotted you here."

Inky meowed softly, sniffing the woman's hand. "She smells funny," he thought. "But she seems friendly!"

The woman took Inky in her arms. "My name is Kendra. Oh, you are a beautiful black cat. I'm so glad I found you! Black cats are very good luck for witches."

Inky's eyes grew wide with surprise. Black cats were a good thing for witches?

"You are a skinny little thing!" she said. "Come home with me. I'll feed you up."

The woman lived in a dear little cottage in the middle of the forest. Her home was full of large cauldrons and old books. She set Inky down on the floor and he went sniffing about the place.

"Don't eat or drink anything!" the woman warned him. "You see, I'm a witch. I am a good witch and my magic won't hurt you, but you might just swallow something that'll turn you bright purple! And we can't have that, can we? A witch's cat must always be jet black – just like you!"

Inky was very happy to hear this. Was he going to be a witch's cat? He didn't dare dream that someone would be happy to have him around, in case he was disappointed again. He had had such bad luck already!

"I can't wait to show you off to the other witches in my coven," Kendra said, picking Inky up and stroking him lovingly. "I am the only witch around who doesn't have a black cat, and my magic has never been as good as it could be. You might just be the stroke of good luck I need!"

Inky was very happy in his new home. He helped the kind witch and accompanied her on all her trips and errands. One night, the witch brought out her flying broomstick from the broom cupboard. "Hold on tight, little one," she said. "We are going on a long ride."

Flying in the night sky was the most thrilling experience Inky had ever had. Their broomstick cut through clouds and soared across the sky. A little while later, Kendra landed the broom next to another, larger, cottage. There they were met by a coven of pretty witches, all gathered around a huge cauldron. In a patch of grass nearby, lots of black cats were playing happily together. Inky walked over to them and watched them, shyly. He had never seen another black cat before, let alone so many at once!

"Kendra! It is lovely to see you again! It's been too long!" said a tall blonde witch, hugging Kendra tightly.

"It's lovely to see you too, Faye," Kendra replied. "I'm sorry it's been a while since I last joined the coven. After the last meeting I attended I felt so disheartened."

"Now, Kendra," said a very strange-looking witch. She had short blue hair and bright-green eyes, with a friendly smile. "I know you've been struggling to cast repairing spells, but that's no reason to hide away. We will help you as much as we can."

"Why thank you, Beth." Kendra turned to Inky, who was licking his paws shyly on the ground, and showed him to her friends. "But look, I've finally found myself a cat!"

All the witches in Kendra's coven cooed at Inky and stroked his jet-black fur. They all commented on Kendra's amazing good fortune to have found him. He was thrilled!

"Now that I have my lovely new cat to give me some magical good luck, I would like to try the repairing spell again," said Kendra.

"Of course!" Faye smiled. "Feel free. Good luck!"

The whole coven waited with bated breath as they watched Kendra create a magic potion in the cauldron. She added herbs and lots of magical ingredients, whispering spells as she stirred the orange liquid first one way, and then another. When she had finished, she filled a small vial with the potion and walked towards a nearby tree that had a broken branch.

She poured the potion onto the branch and

muttered some more spells under her breath. Everyone watched her excitedly, including Inky, who was still standing near the other black cats in the grass. They all waited for the branch to repair itself. They waited and waited, but nothing happened!

Everyone looked at Kendra with sympathy and disappointment. Inky's heart sank and he felt very sad. Perhaps black cats weren't so lucky for witches after all!

"Oh no!" cried Kendra, burying her face in her hands. "It didn't work! I'm a terrible witch!" The other witches consoled her gently.

Suddenly, Inky had an idea. He climbed onto Kendra's shoulder and licked her cheek affectionately. Kendra smiled at him.

"Let me try again," she said to Beth, who was about to empty the cauldron with a flick of her wand. The other witches stepped back and allowed her to use the cauldron once more.

She tried the spell again, this time with Inky on her shoulder, and to her astonishment the tree branch repaired itself and was as good as new!

Everybody cheered loudly.

"I think I can do anything as long as I have Inky here to give me good luck!" said Kendra, hugging him tightly. "Hurray for black cats!"

Inky purred with delight. Finally, he truly felt like he was a very lucky cat. He had a wonderful time living with Kendra and helping her to perform spells and make potions. He made friends with all of the other black cats in the coven. Kendra even took him back to visit the Sedgwicks sometimes, and Inky never felt lonely or unwanted again.

The Winter Circus

Once upon a time in the little town of Gladshire, there lived a young boy who had no mother or father or any other family. All he had was a fine little pet penguin called Pablo. Nobody knew how a penguin from the South Pole had come to Gladshire. Nobody knew where the boy came from, either, and they didn't even know his real name.

Yet, the boy was happier than anyone else in Gladshire. If anyone asked him how his day was going, he would reply: "Everything is tickety-boo!" That's why all the people of Gladshire called him Tickety-Boo. It was a strange name for a boy, but Tickety-Boo didn't mind.

Every day, Tickety-Boo would find new ways to earn money for himself and Pablo. On some days, he would run errands for a coin or two. On other days, he would help thatch someone's roof or pluck the weeds from someone's flowerbed. Everyone was happy to have him, as he could brighten up the day like a ray of sunshine.

One winter morning, Tickety-Boo was shopping in the town square when he heard the town crier ringing his bell. The little boy perked up his ears.

"Hear ye, hear ye!" cried the town crier. "The Winter Circus has come to town, in the clearing just outside the woods. The first show will be at sunset tomorrow!"

All the people in the town square began talking about it. "A circus in the middle of winter?" thought Tickety-Boo. "What a strange idea! I simply must see this circus!"

Tickety-Boo was very curious and felt as though he couldn't wait until the next evening. He rushed to the clearing near the woods, hoping to see the winter circus as it was being set up. He was in luck! As Tickety-Boo walked into the clearing, he spotted a large cluster of caravans to one side, bustling with people. Some women were standing around a large open fire, cooking things in enormous metal pots. Others were hanging out their colourful circus outfits to dry, in time for their first performance. And there were many children running around and playing. Even the toddlers were doing somersaults!

Tickety-Boo spotted a large group of men standing around the huge tent that would be the Big Top. "One... two... three... HEAVE HO!" they shouted as they hoisted it up. Finally, the Big Top rose proudly into the air.

It was nothing like the Big Tops Tickety-Boo had ever seen before. It didn't have any of the usual colourful stripes or showy flags. It was made of rich, brown wool, with white fur trimming. The circus people were catching their breath after all their hard work. Tickety-Boo could see that even in the cold winter air, they were sweating.

"Hello," said Tickety-Boo, walking towards the circus people. "Welcome to Gladshire!"

A tall man with a thick, dark moustache and blue eyes came forward. He had big broad shoulders and looked middle-aged. "Hello, very pleased to meet you," he said with a big smile. "Vhat is your name?"

"Well," said Tickety-Boo, "I'm not quite sure what my name is. But everyone calls me Tickety-Boo."

"Tickety-Boo, you say?" said the circus man. "I am Alexander ze Great – ze owner and ringmaster of zis circus."

"It is a lovely circus, Mr Alexander," said Tickety-Boo.

"Thank you, little boy!" he replied. "Now, it's time for me to get back to vork. But please feel free to look around and talk to the people here."

Tickety-Boo did just that. He ate with the circus people, enjoying some of the most delicious food he had ever tasted. The circus women pushed a large plate of stroganoff into his hand. It was a warm, gooey beef and mushroom stew that was served with crisp bread. He gorged himself on spicy shish kabobs and washed down his meal with a mug of sbiten – a delicious warm drink that was both sweet and spicy, all at the same time.

"This is the best food I've ever tasted!" said Tickety-Boo. "Why, I wish the Winter Circus would stay in Gladshire forever."

The Winter Circus

"I am glad you like eet!" said a voice from behind. It was Alexander once more. "Vould you like to see ze animals?"

"Oh yes, Mr Alexander!" said Tickety-Boo, happily. He followed Alexander deeper into the woods, where there were even more caravans. Unlike the caravans in which the circus people lived, these ones looked like cages with wheels. And inside them were the most beautiful animals Tickety-Boo had ever seen.

He enjoyed watching the playful seals and the sleepy walruses in their caravans. There were ferocious-looking bears and two great tigers, too! A trainer walked by, holding a cute bear cub. It extended its tiny paw and shook hands with Tickety-Boo!

"Don't you have any penguins, Mr Alexander?" asked Tickety-Boo.

"Ve used to," said Alexander. "But not any more. Zey are so rarely found here!"

Bidding goodbye to Alexander and the other circus folk, Tickety-Boo hurried home and told Pablo all about the circus. "Troooooo!" trilled Pablo. He was excited, too! The next day, the two of them made their way to the Winter Circus.

It was a very cold day in Gladshire, and Tickety-Boo had made sure to dress in warm clothes. But inside the Big Top, he felt warm and cosy. Since Tickety-Boo and Pablo were so early, they got the best seats in the front row.

In no time, the Big Top was full of people. Then, all of a sudden, the lights snapped off, leaving everything in darkness. A hush fell over the crowd.

A spotlight came on, focusing on Alexander. He looked dashing in a tuxedo with a red cummerbund around his waist and a top hat upon his head. "Ladies and gentlemen, boys and girls, velcome to ze Vinter Circus!"

Tickety-Boo could barely contain his excitement as Alexander introduced the acts, one after the other. The acrobats and trapeze artists performed breathtaking stunts with ease and grace. The sad-faced clowns were hilarious and the fire-breather made everyone gasp! The crowd ooh-ed and aah-ed throughout the show, completely captivated.

Then Alexander came back on stage. "Now, ladies and gentlemen," he said, "it's time for ze most vonderful, splendid and amazing act of ze night! Behold, ze beautiful circus animals!"

Out came a parade of animals with their trainers, followed by a marching brass bandplaying a lively, happy tune. The audience began to cheer wildly.

Tickety-Boo was amazed. "This is fantastic!" he said, turning to Pablo. "Look how well those tigers are marching, Pablo! Pablo...?"

But the seat next to him was empty. Pablo had gone off somewhere! Tickety-Boo started to panic, but then he saw his little penguin friend squeezing through the barrier and waddling towards the stage.

"Oh dear!" cried Tickety-Boo. "Pablo, come back! You'll get hurt!"

Over all the noise and the music, nobody – least of all Pablo – could hear Tickety-Boo's warnings. Tickety-Boo was beside himself with worry. Pablo was the only family he had. The little penguin walked up to the stage and joined the parade, waving his flippers happily at the crowd.

"Oh, Pablo!" said Tickety-Boo, feeling very relieved and clapping his hands in glee. "What a smart little penguin you are!"

Pablo followed the animals backstage. A few minutes later, he re-emerged, wearing a ruffled collar and balancing on a large beach ball. The audience cheered wildly for Pablo, while Tickety-Boo simply watched in amazement.

Pablo had not finished, however. A trainer threw three small balls towards him and he began juggling them expertly. "My word," exclaimed Tickety-Boo. "I believe that Pablo was meant to be a circus penguin!" Everyone

The Winter Circus

from Gladshire seemed to agree with this. After the show was over, they could not stop congratulating Tickety-Boo for having such a wonderful, talented pet.

Alexander came up to him, too. "Pablo is a natural!" he said. "Vould you let him join ze Vinter Circus?"

"Y–yes, yes of course!" said Tickety-Boo. "If he wants to, I will certainly allow him to join."

It was clear that Pablo *did* want to be part of the circus. He would rehearse with the circus all day and come home to Tickety-Boo at night. This made Tickety-Boo sad, but he tried very hard to hide it.

Soon, the Winter Circus would have to leave Gladshire and go to another town, taking Pablo with them. The little penguin didn't know this yet, of course, but Tickety-Boo did, and he grew very sad.

On the last day of the Winter Circus in Gladshire, Tickety-Boo went to the clearing again. He wanted to spend the whole day with Pablo, even if it meant watching him rehearse all day long.

As Tickety-Boo was watching the penguin

walk around on his flippers, Alexander came and stood next to him and put his arm around his shoulder.

"How are you?" he asked.

"Oh, I'm doing marvellously," he replied. "Everything is tickety... tickety-*BOO-HOO*!" and he burst into tears.

"Oh, don't cry!" said Alexander. "It seems so unlike you to be sad!"

"I will miss Pablo!" sniffled Tickety-Boo.

"I know eet ees difficult to say goodbye, Tickety-Boo," Alexander said. "Vhy don't you join ze Vinter Circus, too?"

"Pah," said Tickety-Boo. "I am not talented like Pablo. Why, I'd be too afraid to do any circus tricks!"

"You can take care of ze animals," suggested Alexander.

"I'd be afraid of them, too!" replied Tickety-Boo. "Thanks for your offer, Alexander – but Gladshire is my home! I know this town like the back of my hand, but I'm afraid that's all I know."

"Very vell," said Alexander, sadly. "If you have made your decision, zhere ees nothing

I can do. But I have something to make you happy again. You can vatch tonight's show from a very special place."

As sad as he was, Tickety-Boo *did* cheer up a little at this idea. They went into the Big Top and he followed Alexander up a very long ladder, finally reaching a high platform.

"The trapeze artists use zis platform," explained Alexander. "It ees very high, so be careful."

"I will, Mr Alexander," said Tickety-Boo. "Thank you so much!"

Even with this amazing view, Tickety-Boo could not really enjoy the circus performances. He didn't even crack a smile when the clowns threw pies at each other! All he could do was wait for Pablo to come on stage.

Finally, the time had come. "Now, ladies and gentlemen," boomed Alexander. "It ees time for an act that has never been seen before. I present to you, the Amazing Pyramid of Animals!"

Two large, sturdy walruses came on stage, balancing on two large balls. Two bear cubs followed and climbed onto their backs. A seal climbed up next, followed by two smaller bear cubs. Another smaller seal made its way up the pile and was held aloft by the bear cubs. And finally, a little creature clambered to the very top, to stand on the seal's back. Can you guess who it was?

"Pablo!" shouted Tickety-Boo, more alarmed than amazed.

"Troo!" replied Pablo, breaking his concentration. In that moment, he slipped on his platform and went tumbling down. But before he could fall too far, two arms locked themselves around him and pulled him up to safety.

It was Tickety-Boo! Seeing Pablo in danger had made him forget all his fear. He had grabbed onto a trapeze with his feet and swung himself towards Pablo, catching him easily.

"Tickety-Boo!" exclaimed Alexander, his voice full of amazement. "How could you do zat?"

"I–I don't know, Mr Alexander," said Tickety-Boo. "It–it was easy!"

"You need lots of practisce before you can do zis kind of trick," said the ringmaster, shaking

The Winter Circus

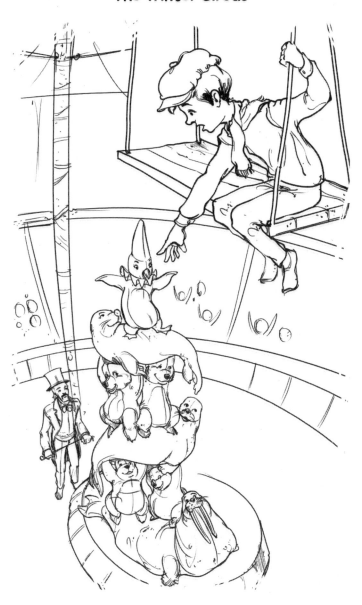

his head. "No, no, no... How can eet be? But vait... eet makes sense!"

"Is something the matter, Mr Alexander?" asked Tickety-Boo, feeling confused.

Alexander sighed, covering his face sadly. "Vell, my boy," he said. "Ten years ago, I lost my leetle son. He was playing in ze voods wiz a baby of one of ze circus penguins. If someone took zem, or if zey ran off, I don't know..."

"That means... I could be your son?" asked Tickety-Boo. He had never imagined that he would ever find his family. "How can we be sure?"

"Vell," said Alexander, stroking his chin. "My son had a red birthmark on his right arm. Do you have one?"

Tickety-Boo was speechless. He rolled up the right sleeve of his jumper, and there it was – a big, red birthmark on his arm!

"My son!" cried Alexander, tears trickling down his face. "Mikhail!"

The two of them hugged and kissed while everyone clapped and cheered. What a beautiful reunion it was!

"Father," said Tickety-Boo, still testing the

The Winter Circus

word on his tongue. "Does this mean I can travel in the circus with you?"

"Yes," said Alexander. "And vhen I am old and retired, you vill become ze new ringmaster of ze Vinter Circus."

Tickety-Boo was overjoyed. He slowly but surely learnt all the tricks of the trade from his father and enjoyed his life in the circus. And when he introduced himself, he always said: "I'm Mikhail, but you can call me Tickety-Boo. Everything is just tickety-boo!" And it was!

Trouble in Sweetlandia

Sweetlandia was simply the sweetest town you could ever find. The entire town was made completely of sweets and candy of all kinds. The fences were made of thick liquorice; the walls, of gingerbread; and the cobblestones, of gumdrops!

The streets were lined with sweet shops of different kinds. There were shops for cakes, boiled sweets and jellies. Some shops sold toys made of candies. There were even shops where you could buy furniture made of sweets!

But the Sweetlandians couldn't live on sweets alone, now, could they? Whenever they were in the mood for a different taste, they would go to one of the non-sweet shops. Paprika the pixie had a shop with a café called Spicy Scraps. She sold all kinds of spicy food there. Mr Lemon had one too. It was called Tangy Treats, and it sold sour foods that made

Trouble in Sweetlandia

the Sweetlandians' tongues tingle.

Finally, there was a dwarf named Bitters who sold only bitter foods in his shop, Bitter Bites. Cooking bitter foods had made him quite bitter! The happy people of Sweetlandia found it hard to get along with Bitters, who was cross all the time.

Paprika and Mr Lemon were happy with their businesses. But Bitters was not. "Nobody ever comes to my shop," he grumbled. "Paprika and Mr Lemon have plenty of customers! Why doesn't anybody come to Bitter Bites?" Of course he didn't realise that whenever he snapped and snarled at customers, it made them vow to never return again.

One day, while he was polishing the tabletops in his little café, an elf walked in. He plopped himself on a chair and started looking through the menu.

"Ah!" said Bitters, brightening up. "A customer! I hope he orders a lot of food."

Bitters went up to the elf.

"So what do you want?" he said. "Have you come to eat or just to gaze at the menu all day?"

The little elf was taken aback.

"Hello," he replied, timidly. "I'd like bitter coffee, please. No sugar."

"Is that all?" asked Bitters. "Are you sure you wouldn't like a whole meal? Our bitter melon salad is quite delicious..."

"No, thank you," said the elf. "I'll just have a coffee. I'm meeting a friend for lunch at Spicy Scraps!"

Upon hearing this, Bitters nearly threw a fit! "My shop is as good as Paprika's!" he said. "Why can't you eat here?"

"M–m–my friend isn't very fond of bitter food!" the elf stammered, alarmed at how violent Bitters sounded. "Otherwise, I'd have loved to eat here!"

"Pah!" spat Bitters angrily. "Nobody has good taste around here."

He stomped off angrily to fetch the coffee, leaving the poor elf very distressed at his outburst. The elf drank his coffee as soon as he could, paid his bill and rushed off. He didn't want Bitters to yell at him again!

Meanwhile, Bitters could not calm himself down.

"Bitter Bites should be the only non-sweet shop in all of Sweetlandia!" he said. "I'm going to find a way to make sure Spicy Scraps and Tangy Treats have to shut their doors forever."

And so Bitters began to plot. The next day, he chopped off his long beard and smoothed his hair down with grease. Then he rubbed soot all over his hair, turning it jet black. Lastly he put on a pair of thick spectacles and a neat jacket and tie.

"Perfect. Even I can't recognise myself!" he said, looking into the mirror with satisfaction. "I am all set for my lunch at Spicy Scraps. Oh! But I have one last thing to do."

He went to the mouse traps that he had set up in the different corners of his house. He put all the mice that had been caught into a large bag and zipped it up. Then he made his way to Spicy Scraps. He could barely see a thing through his thick spectacles.

Bumbling along as if he were blind, Bitters finally managed to enter Paprika's shop.

"Hello!" said Paprika, pleasantly. "Have a seat, won't you? Here is the menu."

"Uh, hello," said Bitters. He sat at the table and held the menu, unable to read anything. Bitters squinted at Paprika through his thick spectacles.

"Sir…" said Paprika, hesitantly. "You're holding the menu upside down. Would you like me to tell you what the specials are?"

Bitters managed to place his order thanks to Paprika's help. When she went into the kitchen to prepare his food, Bitters put his mean plan into action. He unzipped his bag and let the mice out into Paprika's shop.

Bitters sniggered. "Now let's see how many people choose Spicy Scraps over Bitter Bites!" he said. The mice scattered about the floor.

Just then, Paprika came back, holding a

tray with his food.

"Oh!" she exclaimed. "What are these huge clumps of dust flying about? Why, I thought they were mice!"

Bitters was confused. "They *are* mice!" he said.

"No, sir," said Paprika kindly. "They're only dust bunnies. Take a closer look. I would never have mice in my shop."

The dwarf took off his glasses in a hurry. Paprika was right! "Silly me!" Bitters muttered under his breath. "I didn't see what I was doing! I must have just collected dust bunnies from the empty cages. Oh, bother!"

Bitters was upset with himself. He'd messed up his own plan!

He ate his meal, paid the bill and walked out in a huff. "Tomorrow I'll try my luck at Mr Lemon's shop," he said to himself. "I can come back to Paprika's later."

This time, Bitters came up with a slightly different plan. He wore the same disguise as last time – but without the thick glasses! And instead of mice, Bitters took a piece of old, smelly fish and put it in a bag. It really did let off a dreadful stink!

Bitters had decided that he would put it on his plate and claim that it came from the kitchen! All the customers would see it. And Mr Lemon's reputation would be ruined.

But as Bitters entered the café, all the other customers looked over in his direction, wrinkling their noses. They could tell that the dreadful smell was coming from him!

Mr Lemon, a sharp but kindly soul, immediately came up to Bitters' table. He also realised that it was Bitters who smelt so awful.

"Sir," he said calmly. "Would you mind having a seat out on the deck? I'd be happy to serve you there."

Bitters was embarrassed.

"N–never mind," he said hastily. He turned away and hurried out before anyone could recognise him. His plan had backfired once again.

Back at Bitter Bites, Bitters was sullenly mopping the floors when a customer opened the shop door. Hearing the bell tinkle, Bitters looked up hopefully, but it was only the little elf from the other day.

"You again," said Bitters, miserably. "All you will drink is black coffee!"

"Oh, cheer up," said the elf. "We are Sweetlandians! How can you be so glum when you live in such a cheery town? Come now; tell me what the matter is. I might be able to help."

"You're an elf, aren't you? That means that you can help me with your magic, right?" asked Bitters. "Then help me magic away Paprika and Mr Lemon's shops! I want to be the only non-sweet shop in Sweetlandia."

"That's easy," said the elf. "Why, you can do it yourself!" He slipped two small bells on the table.

"What are these?" asked Bitters grumpily.

"They're magical!" said the elf. "Drop one bell in Spicy Scraps and the other in Tangy Treats. Both Paprika and Mr Lemon will move away in no time!"

Bitters' eyes shone greedily. This sounded like a fine plan.

"You've been useful to me, after all!" he said. "I'll go and drop the bells tonight. Tomorrow I will see if your magic is real."

The elf only smiled in reply.

That night, Bitters dropped the bells through the windows of both shops. He tiptoed back home and had a good night's sleep.

In the morning, Bitters woke up and rushed over to see Paprika. To his utmost delight, she was packing all her things into her suitcase.

"Hello, Paprika," he called. "I see you're moving away."

"Yes, Bitters," said Paprika. "I decided that I would like a shop that's away from the din –

and earlier this morning, I found the perfect place!"

"Oh!" said Bitters, his smile growing wider. "Is it very far from Sweetlandia?"

"No, of course not!" replied Paprika. "I couldn't dream of leaving Sweetlandia. I am going to move to Mr Lemon's shop, and he's happy to take my spot!"

Bitters' smile turned into a scowl. Oh no! Nothing was going his way. From the corner of his eye, he spotted the elf laughing at him from the bushes.

"You tricked me!" said Bitters, bitterly.

"No," replied the elf. "I was just teaching you a lesson! Instead of trying to put others down, maybe you should try being nicer and think of some ideas for new dishes. Then more people will come to your shop." And the elf somersaulted away into the distance, never to be seen again.

"Blimey," said Bitters, still in shock. "Being jealous and selfish has got me nowhere – and now I've lost my only customer!"

"Why don't you try being nice instead?" said Paprika, who had overheard everything that was going on outside her shop.

"My name is Bitters," spat Bitters. "And my shop is called Bitter Bites. Do you really think I could be anything but bitter and mean?"

"Well, I'm supposed to be feisty and spicy," replied Paprika. "But I can also be sweet. A good dish is all about balance of flavour. That rule works for people, too."

Bitters went home with Paprika's words still playing in his head. When Bitters next cooked his bitter melon salad, he added a pinch of pepper, a splash of lemon and a sprinkle of sugar. It tasted much, much better than his old recipe.

"The flavours all blend into each other and make the salad taste delicious," he said. "Perhaps Paprika was right about the balance of flavours. Well, I *do* live in Sweetlandia. I probably could afford to be a little sweeter."

Bitter tried to be nicer to his customers. At times he was feisty, and, at other times, he was mellow. As for Bitters' bitter side? He saved that only for unruly customers who created a ruckus – and of course, anyone who smelt like rotting fish!

Popular Rewards

And before long, he too had a long line of people coming to his restaurant to taste the unusual food he made every day.

The
Mayor's Cape

Taffeta was a wonderful seamstress who lived in the little town of Hogglepot. She could sew so well that you couldn't even see the stitches on the clothes she made! But what made Taffeta's clothes even more special were the magic touches that she gave them. She made coats that could change colours, trousers with magical pockets that an elephant could fit inside, and even ties that could hold your coffee cup!

If you didn't want any magic in your clothes – too bad! All of Taffeta's clothes were enchanted in one way or another. Taffeta didn't tell people how their clothes were enchanted. She let people figure it out for themselves. She loved giving people surprises. Her surprises were always playful and never mean.

One day, Rico the gnome went to Taffeta

to buy a hat. "I want a hat made of white velvet," he explained, "with purple trim. It should be shaped like a unicorn's head, and the horn should be at least a metre long. Oh, also, please make it glow, if you could!"

"Hmm!" said Taffeta. "This is going to be a task! Come back in a week, and I'll have it ready."

The next week, Rico returned, bouncing up and down. He was very excited about his new hat and couldn't wait to see it!

"Hallo!" said Taffeta. "Your hat is ready. Let me get it for you."

The seamstress brought out a small hatbox and presented it to Rico, who looked at it suspiciously. It was far too small to hold the hat that he had in mind! Where had she put the unicorn horn? He opened the box and gasped in shock.

"This is absolutely not what I asked for!" he said. "It's brown and frumpy and... is that a patched-up hole? Taffeta, I'm afraid I don't like it one bit!"

Taffeta kept a straight face. "Rico, this is *exactly* what you asked for," she said. "Besides, how do you know that you don't like it? You haven't even tried it on!"

Rico did not want to upset Taffeta. He tried the hat on and looked at himself in the mirror. Just as before, it was plain and brown and *not* what he had asked for.

"I can't lie, Taffeta," he said. "I'm not too pleased with this hat."

"But why aren't you happy?" asked Taffeta. "Isn't this what you wanted?"

"Not at all," said Rico. "I wanted a white velvet hat with purple trim, shaped like a unicorn's head with a long horn, and... GOODNESS ME!"

As Rico was speaking, the hat – the brown, frumpy, plain hat on his head – was slowly changing into a white, velvet, unicorn-shaped one! The gnome was ecstatic.

"Oh, Taffeta!" he cried. "You're such a prankster!"

Taffeta giggled, happy to see that Rico was pleased at last.

"It's a magic hat, Rico," she said. "It will become whatever you want it to. All you have to do is tell it what to change into! And when

you take it off, it will turn back into its frumpy, brown self – you'll have the right hat for every outfit now, and no one but you and I will ever know that it's always the same one!"

Rico could not stop thanking Taffeta. He was going to look fabulous at Hogglepot's annual celebration!

Every year, the town celebrated with a huge parade and a party that lasted all night. Preparations were in full swing. The gnomes were standing on one another's shoulders, hanging up bunting and colourful streamers. The pixies were busy making food for the guests and the fairies were sweeping and cleaning the town.

As for Taffeta, her job was to design the

mayor's outfit. Every year she would design something more fantastic than the previous year.

The previous year, Taffeta had dressed the mayor in a tuxedo made of shimmering stardust, which swirled around all night long. Nobody could take his or her eyes off him! The year before that, she had made him a shirt that had long, billowing sleeves. When the mayor flapped his sleeves, he rose up into the air. Everyone was so surprised when they saw their mayor soaring over the parade!

Each year everyone waited with bated breath to see what wondrous design Taffeta would come up with this time around; everyone except Angora, the other seamstress in town. Angora was not as good at sewing as Taffeta. To make things worse, she was also rude and lazy. That's why everyone in Hogglepot preferred going to Taffeta's shop instead. This made Angora very, very jealous. So jealous in fact that she hatched a plan to steal the mayor's outfit from Taffeta.

The night before the parade, Angora crept into Taffeta's shop while she was asleep.

As she tiptoed through the darkened room, Angora spotted an outfit on a dummy right in the middle of the shop. "This *must* be it!" she thought, and she quickly bundled it into a sack that she had brought with her and disappeared into the night.

"Ha! Now that silly old Taffeta will be the laughing stock of the town!" said Angora, cackling wickedly to herself.

When Taffeta woke up the next morning, she was upset to see that the outfit had been stolen. But instead of getting upset, she stayed calm and simply smiled. "I'm sure everything will be back in order soon enough," she thought to herself.

Meanwhile, back at home, Angora took a good look at the mayor's outfit. It was nothing but a simple blue cape!

"Hmph!" she scoffed. "What a terrible, unimaginative outfit. I could have made something much better."

Nonetheless, Angora tried the cape on, thinking that a simple cape would come in handy. As soon as she did this, the cape did a strange thing. It began to wrinkle and shrink, and it turned blacker than the blackest soot!

"Yuck!" gasped Angora, struggling to remove it. "It smells awful!" And, truly, the cape was giving off a dreadful smell. It kept getting blacker and more wrinkled, almost as if it was rotting!

Angora threw off the cape and rushed upstairs to have a bath. But no matter how hard she scrubbed herself, the rotting smell would not wash off!

"That Taffeta!" she spat. "Thanks to her and her horrible cape, I shall smell like a rubbish bin at the parade!"

When Angora came out of her bathroom, the stink had spread to her whole house!

"The neighbours will certainly smell this and wonder what smells so bad," cried Angora. "What was Taffeta thinking? The mayor will hate this horrid cape!"

Angora didn't know what to do. She sprayed perfume all over her home and the cape to mask the horrid smell. But it just wouldn't go away!

As everyone was getting ready for the parade and beginning to gather in the town

square, they couldn't help but notice a strange
and terrible pong! It seemed to be coming from
Angora's house.

"Oh goodness, somebody should do
something!" cried the town's residents. "The
parade is going to begin any minute. We can't
have the whole town smelling dreadful!"

Taffeta went to Angora's house to try to
fix the matter. She knew very well what the
smell was. After all, it was her who'd made it
happen!

"Hallo, Angora," she said, knocking on her
door. "Don't try to hide away. I already know
you stole the cape."

Angora opened the door just a crack and
pulled Taffeta inside.

"Please do something!" she cried. "I am
sorry! I was jealous and I made a horrible
mistake!"

"It's all right," said Taffeta, mildly. "Now,
give me the cape. The parade has already
begun!"

"But it's so horrible and smelly!" said
Angora. "Why would the mayor want to wear
it?"

The Mayor's Cape

"You'll see," Taffeta said mysteriously. She scooped up the cape and dashed to the mayor's office, where the parade usually began. Angora followed her. She couldn't believe that Taffeta was truly going to give the awful cape to the major!

The streets were lined with townspeople. They all held their noses when Taffeta passed by. "Ugh!" they said. "What ever is that smell?"

The mayor was sitting on his float, waiting anxiously for Taffeta. The mayor always led the parade, and the festivities could not begin until he was ready, wearing his special new clothes.

When he saw Taffeta approaching, he was so relieved. But as she got closer, he noticed that the foul smell that seemed to have been hanging about the town all morning was getting worse.

"What on earth is going on, Taffeta?" he asked. "Are you trying one of your silly tricks again? This time you've gone too far!"

"Not at all, Mayor," said the seamstress. "If you would just try it on…"

"Never!" exclaimed the mayor. "I can't wear that. It smells dreadful – and looks even worse!"

"It's no ordinary cape, Mayor," explained Taffeta. "It's a cape that shows your true colours. If you are a mean person, the cape will shrivel up, rot and smell terrible. But if you are a good person, the cape will show your true qualities."

Angora blushed in embarrassment. She felt ashamed about how mean and spiteful she had become and how horrid she had been, not just towards Taffeta, but to everyone in Hogglepot. The mayor, on the other hand, was willing to believe that the cape could behave just as Taffeta said. He finally accepted the cape and tied it over his shoulders.

The effect was instantaneous. The black, smelly, shrivelled fabric transformed into a rich, velvety plum-coloured cape, fit for a king! The crowd began to cheer loudly, and the mayor took his seat on the float as the marching band began to play a merry tune.

Then, something even more fantastic happened. As the mayor raised his cape to

The Mayor's Cape

wave at the townspeople, strings of pearls and jewels flew out from the cape! The crowd cheered and shouted with joy.

"Taffeta, you truly are a genius!" said the happy mayor. "Please join me on my float."

"With pleasure, Mayor!" beamed Taffeta, climbing up onto it. What an amazing view! Throngs of people were happily collecting jewels and marvelling at their good fortune. She even spotted Rico, wearing his splendid unicorn hat!

"Thank you, Mayor!" Rico smiled. "Thank you, Taffeta!"

A little further along, Taffeta saw Angora in the crowd, looking shamefaced. Everyone knew what she had done, and they were all ignoring her. Taffeta, however, was so kind-hearted that she believed that everyone had goodness inside themselves somewhere. She got off the float to comfort Angora.

To her surprise, Angora spoke first. "I realise that I've been a bad person," she said. "But I'm hoping I can change. Instead of being jealous of you, I would like to help you and learn from you, Taffeta. Will you allow me to

128

work in your shop?"

"What a great idea!" said Taffeta. "I could certainly use the help! Come on, let's join the dancing."

Hand-in-hand, the two seamstresses ran to join the party. They danced all night. It was the best ball that Hogglepot had ever had.

From then on Taffeta learnt how to make wonderful, magical clothes. They came up with many new ideas, like shoelaces that tied themselves, a bib that wiped your mouth after each bite, and t-shirts that turned into warm fleecy jumpers whenever it got cold! Now that Angora was putting her energies to good use she was a fast learner. Soon, she was just as good as Taffeta!

Time flew by, and soon, nearly a year had passed. Hogglepot had once again begun preparing for its annual party. Taffeta and Angora went to the mayor's home to measure him for his new outfit. When they were finished, Angora had a question.

"Mayor," she said. "If you still have your cape from last year, may I try it on?"

"Of course!" said the kind mayor. He

brought out the cape from his closet and passed it to Angora.

This time, when Angora tried it on, it did not shrivel up and stink. Instead, it transformed into a beautiful pink silk cloak that showered velvety rose petals whenever it moved!

Taffeta beamed at her friend. "You've come such a long way," she said. "I am so proud of you."

Angora and Taffeta became the best of friends and made the people of Hogglepot wonderful clothes for many, many years.

The
Shoe Tree

Ballyhoo was a naughty little brownie. He loved playing tricks on all the people in the village. He would steal people's shoes, tie the laces together, and then fling them up into the big apple tree that stood in the middle of the village.

In fact, Ballyhoo had played this trick so many times that the tree began to look as if it was growing lots and lots of shoes, rather than apples! There were big shoes and little shoes, shoes made of leather and shoes made of wood. Ballyhoo had gathered quite a collection!

The village people had all learnt to keep their shoe cupboards locked at all times, but that didn't stop Ballyhoo! He would always find one way or another to get his hands on people's shoes. One day, he was walking by the park when he saw a little fairy learning to fly for the first time. As she lifted off the ground, her little shoes fell off her feet. SWOOP! Ballyhoo charged in and ran off with her shoes before she even realised they were off.

"Hee, hee, hee!" giggled Ballyhoo as he ran towards the tree. "I've got her shoes! I've got her shoes!"

"Ballyhoo!" scolded Mr Kent, who was passing by. "How will that poor fairy walk home without her shoes?"

"Hoo, hoo, hoo!" laughed Ballyhoo. "I suppose she has no choice but to learn how to fly now!" He never felt sorry about his actions. Everyone in the village was quite tired of trying to make him understand that what he was doing was wrong.

One day, though, Ballyhoo went a little too far with his trickery. There was a new elf in town, called Tinkletoes, and everyone was talking about him. This was because Tinkletoes was extremely fashionable. No one ever saw him with even a single hair out of place. He wore the finest green tailored suits. His cufflinks were made of emeralds and his hat of moss-green velvet.

Ballyhoo first met Tinkletoes in the street.

The Shoe Tree

The elf was having a conversation with Mr Kent when Ballyhoo walked up to them.

"Hello," said Ballyhoo. "Who do we have here?"

"This is Tinkletoes," said Mr Kent. "Tinkletoes, this is Ballyhoo."

"Pleased to meet you, Ballyhoo," said Tinkletoes.

"Oh, the pleasure is – MY WORD!" Ballyhoo's eyes went straight to Tinkletoes' feet. They were the most beautiful shoes that

the brownie had ever seen – crafted from the softest brown leather and sewn so finely that you couldn't even see the seams. They tapered to a point at the toes and ended in two bright golden bells that chimed musically when Tinkletoes walked.

"Be careful around Ballyhoo," said Mr Kent. "He's eyeing your shoes. He's the one responsible for the shoe tree that you saw in the middle of the village."

"Oh, so *you're* the notorious shoe thief," said Tinkletoes with a small smile. "Don't worry, Mr Kent. I'll make sure that my shoes stay firmly on my feet."

"Hoo, hoo, hoo," laughed Ballyhoo, mischievously. "We'll see about that!"

Over the next few days, Ballyhoo tried very hard to steal Tinkletoes' shoes. But Tinkletoes didn't have a shoe cupboard near his front door. He didn't go swimming, jump on trampolines or do anything else that would require him to take off his shoes. Ballyhoo felt completely helpless. He went home and thought up a mischievous plan to steal Tinkletoes' shoes.

The Shoe Tree

One balmy night, Ballyhoo crept out of his cottage and tiptoed to Tinkletoes' home. "Ah!" whispered Ballyhoo to himself. "He's left his window open. I knew he would – it's much too warm tonight."

Grabbing on to the creepers that grew on the walls, Ballyhoo climbed up the side of the house easily and went in through Tinkletoes' window. It was very dark, but Ballyhoo could just about make out the shape of the sleeping elf. He was snoring loudly, his chest rising and falling with each snore.

Ballyhoo waited for his eyes to adjust to the darkness. Once that was done, it was as easy as pie to spot the beautiful pair of shoes. Their golden bells shone brightly, even in the darkness.

In a flash, Ballyhoo grabbed the shoes and ran to the window as quietly as he could. But the foolish brownie had forgotten that the shoes made a sound, too. The two bells began tinkling loudly, of their own accord, waking up Tinkletoes.

"Who's that?" called Tinkletoes. "Thief! Thief!"

Ballyhoo didn't waste a moment. He clambered out of the window and down the creepers, the bells ringing loudly all the while. He ran to the shoe tree, tied the laces of the shoes together, and hurled the shoes up into the branches. They swung around wildly for a few moments and then stopped. The bells fell silent, too. Ballyhoo ran home, feeling very pleased with himself.

The next morning, Tinkletoes looked very cross. He had a big frown on his face and his toes were no longer tinkling. He had on another pair of shoes – still very pretty, but not as beautiful as his first pair. All the villagers knew that his shoes had been stolen by Ballyhoo. He was furious.

The Shoe Tree

Ballyhoo, however, was not apologetic in the least. On the contrary, he was quite pleased with himself. He skipped around the village cheerily, doffing his hat to everyone that passed him by. Ballyhoo didn't even have to boast of his achievement – it was up on the shoe tree for all to see. But when he tried to doff his hat to Mr Kent, he received a knock on the head with a walking stick!

"Breaking into someone's private home?" shouted Mr Kent. "Why, you ought to be thrown in prison! It's very kind of Tinkletoes not to take you straight to the police."

"Pah!" scoffed Ballyhoo. "You can't prove anything."

"Well, remember this," said Mr Kent. "Someone could be watching you! And then you will have to pay."

At that very moment, Tinkletoes was passing by. When he heard Mr Kent's words, a small smile appeared on his pointed face. Yes, he was going to make Ballyhoo pay. And how he would pay!

A few days later, Ballyhoo was itching to get his hands on someone's shoes once more. He roamed around the village, looking for a good target. He spotted an elderly man who was trying to get on the bus. Ballyhoo rubbed his hands together in glee. He was going to snatch his shoes at the very last minute!

Giggling to himself, he raced towards the man. And just then, a strange tinkling noise came to his ears. It sounded just like the bells on Tinkletoes' shoes, but was much, much louder.

"Look, the shoes on the shoe tree are moving!" said a passer-by. Ballyhoo turned to look. He couldn't quite believe it! The shoes were beginning to move like mouths, with their insoles acting as tongues. "Hold on to your shoes!" cried the shoes. "Ballyhoo is on the loose!"

The brownie stopped in his tracks. The villagers turned to look at him angrily and backed away. The old man placed his feet firmly on the ground. There went Ballyhoo's chance to steal his shoes!

"D–don't listen to those silly shoes," said Ballyhoo. "They've been hanging up there for far too long!"

The Shoe Tree

But the shoe tree had not finished with him. One by one, the shoes unwound themselves from the branches of the trees and began to walk in the street, as cool as can be. Leading the procession was Tinkletoes' handsome pair, the bells ringing gallantly. Frightened, Ballyhoo ran home and hid.

The villagers could not stop staring. "They seem to be making their way to Ballyhoo's cottage," one of them whispered.

Sure enough, the first few pairs of shoes walked straight up to Ballyhoo's front door. Tinkletoes' shoes rapped on the door with all their might. When Ballyhoo opened it, he was in for a shock! Before he could say anything, the shoes all leapt in the air and began slapping him.

"Ouch! Oh!" cried Ballyhoo. He tried to escape, but the shoes blocked his doorway. He tried to climb out of a window, but there were shoes there, too! The naughty brownie only realised what was really happening when he saw Tinkletoes appear at his door with a smile on his face. Tinkletoes was using magic to make the shoes move!

The Shoe Tree

"Tinkletoes! Oh, please make this stop!" said Ballyhoo. "It was only a joke!"

"Is that so?" asked Tinkletoes. Suddenly, Ballyhoo felt the slaps becoming harder.

"Please, make it stop, Tinkletoes!" said Ballyhoo. "Oh, I am ever so sorry that I stole your shoes – and everyone else's!"

"Will you promise not to do it again?" said Tinkletoes.

"Yes, yes!" said Ballyhoo. "Just make them stop!"

Tinkletoes snapped his fingers. All at once, the shoes fell to the floor, lifeless. With another snap, they all lined up and marched out of the door. Ballyhoo watched in awe as they made their way back to their owners.

"Remember, Ballyhoo, I will be watching. If you try to steal someone's shoes again, this will keep happening to you."

It was a long time before Ballyhoo felt the urge to steal anyone else's shoes. Whenever the thought even crept into his mind, he would hear a certain tinkling sound that made him quickly forget all about it!

Blundering
Buddies

Juniper was a dear little genie who loved to grant people's wishes. But she could never quite get them right! She was always mixing up spells and making a huge mess.

One day, Tanglebeard the dwarf knocked upon Juniper's door.

"Juniper, I have a problem," he said. "I have to go to a party tomorrow and I want to have the longest beard there. I need to grow it by at least 30 centimetres. Can you make my wish come true?"

"Yes, yes, of course!" said Juniper, clapping her hands with joy. Granting wishes for others made her truly happy.

"Now, let's see..." muttered Juniper to herself. "Hmm, 30 centimetres – that's about a foot, isn't it? So, now, which spell should I use? Aha! I know just the one!"

Juniper cleared her throat and began

twirling her fingers.

"Pixie dust, ash and soot,
Make this beard grow a foot!"

For a minute, nothing happened. Then Tanglebeard's long beard began to sparkle and glow!

"It's working!" cried Juniper. "I did it!"

But Juniper *hadn't* done it. Instead of growing a foot longer, Tanglebeard's beard had sprouted an actual foot, complete with five hairy toes!

"Oh, Juniper, what have you done?" wailed Tanglebeard, looking at his beard in horror. "I'll look like a fool at the party now!"

"I'm ever so sorry!" said Juniper hastily. "I can try to fix it."

"No!" said Tanglebeard, shaking his head. "No, don't try anything! You might make it worse. I will go to the genie in the next town."

Tanglebeard hurried out, clutching the foot growing out of his beard. Juniper was awfully disappointed.

Later, Dame Daffodil came by with a broken walking stick. "Juniper, dear," she said, "will you fix my walking stick? It's broken and I'm

just too slow without it!"

"Yes, Dame Daffodil!" said Juniper. "I'll fix it in a jiffy."

Juniper narrowed her eyes with concentration. She absolutely did not want to make another blunder! Twirling her fingers, she said:

"Pixies green and fairies blue,
Make this stick strong and true!"

In an instant, the broken walking stick snapped back into one single piece. "Thank you, Juniper!" said Dame Daffodil. "Now I can go to the market with ease – oh!"

Dame Daffodil had tried to pick up her walking stick, but she simply couldn't. Juniper tried, too. She pulled with both arms until she fell over! "I'm sorry, Dame Daffodil," said Juniper, looking dejected. "It's so heavy, it won't budge – I think my spell made it *too* strong!"

Dame Daffodil sighed. "Juniper, you're such a blunderer," she said. "It's all right. I'll just buy another walking stick. I have to hurry now, or the market will close before I get there."

Juniper watched Dame Daffodil walk away slowly. She left her stick still standing upright in the middle of Juniper's living room. She couldn't do anything about it.

"Oh bother! I shouldn't be a genie any longer!" she said to herself sorrowfully. "I only make everything worse! I must stay out of everyone's way."

Just then, she had an idea. "Why don't I bottle myself up?" she thought. "Nobody will find me for a very, very long time. Yes! I think I'll do just that!"

So Juniper packed all her bags and stuffed them into an amber bottle. She then squeezed into it herself, and asked her friend, the eagle, to carry her to a faraway lake.

The eagle carried the bottle with its talons. It flew far, far away, searching for a nice lake for Juniper to live in. Finally, it found one. It loosened its grip, and – *PLOP!* – the bottle fell right into the lake.

At first, Juniper was very happy in the lake. "Ah!" she said. "No more blunders for me!"

But soon, she started to feel very, very lonely. Juniper loved to be with other people.

She missed her friends dearly, and she missed granting wishes, even if they never did come out quite right! Poor Juniper could not perform any magic from inside the bottle. She hoped someone would come soon and set her free.

In the town next to the lake, there lived a little girl called Betty, who was just like Juniper. She was always making blunders! On that particular day, Betty was having a dreadful day.

It had not started out too badly. In fact, Betty's science teacher had given the class some good news that morning.

"We are having a science fair next month," he had said. "Everyone must invent something and show it at the fair. The best invention will win a big prize."

Betty was excited. If she could make a good invention, maybe she could prove to everyone that she didn't always get everything wrong. "I hope I don't make a blunder of this!" she thought.

But then, something absolutely horrid happened to Betty after school, while she was playing football with her friends. Betty was standing on the field, daydreaming, when the ball whizzed towards her feet.

For a moment, she was stunned. She didn't quite realise what was happening!

"Come on, Betty! Dribble the ball!" shouted her friends.

"Oh!" replied Betty, snapping out of her thoughts. She dribbled the football right across the field, dodging whoever came her way. When the goalposts were in sight, she shot the ball, right into the net!

"GOAL!" shouted Betty in excitement. But when she turned around to her teammates, she saw that they were all looking crossly at her. The players on the other team were pointing at her and laughing heartily. Carol, the captain of Betty's team, marched up to her, looking furious.

"You silly girl!" she exploded. "You shot the ball into our own goal! That's a goal for the other team!"

Betty went red with embarrassment. "I–I'm so, so sorry!" she stammered, horrified at her own silly mistake.

Blundering Buddies

The coach came to Betty's rescue. "Come on now," he said. "We all make mistakes! Even so, you showed some very good dribbling skills. Cheer up!"

But Betty *couldn't* cheer up. Even though the coach said it didn't matter, her teammates were still cross. "Oh, I don't know what's worse!" thought Betty. "Half of my class hates me, and the other half can't stop laughing at me."

Betty changed out of her football kit and went back to class, feeling sad. A few boys and girls were looking at her and giggling.

"Blundering Betty," snorted one of the children. "It has a nice ring to it, don't you think?" All his friends began to laugh. Soon, the name spread all over the class. By the end of the day, everyone knew Betty as Blundering Betty.

She trudged home alone, trying very hard not to cry. "What will I tell Mummy when she asks how my day went?" thought Betty. "Oh, I know she'll try to make me feel better, but I'm just so miserable! I'd better not go back just yet!"

So Betty took the long way home, past the lake instead – the very lake in which Juniper lived! Betty set her bag down and picked up a handful of stones.

But just as she was going to fling the first stone into the lake's calm waters, she heard a voice coming from it!

"Um, hello!" called the voice. "Please don't throw stones at me!"

"W–who's that?" stammered Betty, feeling suddenly rather afraid.

"Oh, don't be frightened of me!" said Juniper. "I am Juniper – a genie who lives in this lake."

"A genie!" exclaimed Betty with delight. "How lovely! Would you please grant me a wish? I wish to stop making blunders!"

Jupiter tinkled with laughter. "I would love to help you, Betty," she said, "but I cannot. Not while I'm trapped in this lake!"

"I can help you get out of the lake!" said Betty, brightly.

"That is very nice of you," said Juniper. "But I am trapped inside a bottle with a large crystal stopper. You would have to dive deep into the lake to find me – and this lake is far too cold and deep for you!"

"Hmm," said Betty, thinking aloud. "Don't worry, Juniper. I will come up with a plan!"

Betty walked back home, thinking hard. "I may not be able to swim in the lake, but I can easily reach the middle of it on a raft. I will ask Mum to help me build one."

When Betty's mother heard her strange request, she smiled. "You've come to the right person," she said. "When I was a little girl, I loved to go rafting with my brothers. I can tell you exactly how to build one."

Betty got to work that very afternoon. First, they went out to the garden shed to see what they might use. Luckily, there was a big pile of bamboo poles and some plastic containers from their last camping trip. In the corner was a jumble of old ropes. Perfect!

Over the next few days Betty would finish her homework quickly after school, and then get to work on the raft. First, she arranged the poles to form a platform. Then she used the rope to tie the poles tightly together. After working, she would go to the lake and spend some time talking with Juniper. They were fast becoming friends!

In no time, Betty had a sturdy raft that could easily carry her weight. Her mother gave her a wooden oar that would help her steer on the water, and a life jacket to wear. They began to visit the lake every day to practise. Soon, Betty could paddle and steer without any help.

"Jolly good, Betty!" said her mother. "You are a natural! I think you'll soon be able to go out on the raft by yourself."

Betty was very happy to hear this. Now she was ready to rescue Juniper.

"Bravo, Betty!" said Juniper, on seeing her friend paddling towards the centre of the lake. "Still, this raft is not enough to rescue me. There is no way you will be able to see my bottle from up there!"

"You're right!" said Betty, feeling a little deflated. "I hadn't thought about that!"

"I believe in you, Betty," said Juniper. "You managed to get to the middle of the lake, and now I'm sure you will find a way to reach me, too!"

Blundering Buddies

Betty was very glum. At school the next day, she was hardly paying attention in science class.

"...a periscope helps you see things that are not in front of your eyes," the teacher was saying. "So if you are at a concert and there is a tall person in front of you, a periscope would help you see over their head without having to stretch or crane your neck."

This made Betty's ears perk up! At the end of the class, she eagerly bounded over to her teacher's desk.

"If a pepperscope can be used to see above me, is there an instrument I can use to see beneath me?" she asked her teacher.

Her teacher laughed. "Firstly, it is a *peri*scope," he said. "Secondly, there is a special type of instrument, just like a periscope, that will help you see what is beneath you if you look underwater. It is called a *bathyscope*. You can even use a bathyscope to look at things deep underwater." He was amused at Betty's questions, but happy that she seemed to be taking such an interest in science.

This was exactly what Betty wanted to hear!

She ran back home to her father, who loved to do woodwork in his spare time and was very good with his hands.

"Daddy, I need your help to make a bathyscope," said Betty. "It is an instrument that will help me see underwater!"

Betty's father was surprised to hear her request. But he was delighted that she was showing an interest in his hobby. He found a blueprint with some instructions to make a bathyscope, and they got to work.

The bathyscope was a lot more difficult to make than the raft had been. There was lots of measuring to do and even some work involving glass and mirrors! Betty could not perform the dangerous tasks like cutting and handling glass, so her father did them for her. But Betty did most of the work. She even assembled the whole thing!

After days of hard work, the bathyscope was ready. Betty carried it to the lake and set it on her raft, which was tied to the shore. Then, she paddled herself to the middle of the lake.

"What have you got now?" asked Juniper, curiously.

"Something that will help me look into the darkest depths of the lake!" said Betty. She set the bathyscope carefully on the surface of the lake and pressed a button on its side. Immediately, the bathyscope extended itself down below the surface of the water.

Betty peeked into the glass viewfinder and gasped. She could see a whole underwater world through it! There were schools of tiny fish and beautiful underwater plants. Betty even spotted little turtles floating about happily.

"Oh my," she said to Juniper. "Why would you want to leave this beautiful lake?"

"Well, it is very pretty down here, I suppose," Juniper replied. "But oh, I miss my friends so! I want to go back to them. Can you see my amber bottle?"

"Oh yes, there you are!" said Betty, gleefully. "What a pretty bottle you live in!"

"You can have the bottle once I'm out of it," said Juniper. "But how will you fish me out?"

"I will need another contraption for that," said Betty, feeling slightly crestfallen. But then she thought of something and brightened up: "But don't worry, I have an idea!"

Betty went back home and asked her mother for the keys to the garden shed. There, she spotted a big old butterfly net with a long handle.

"This is not long enough," thought Betty. "But I know what to do!"

She got some of the bamboo poles and rope that was left over from building the raft. Working all by herself, she attached the bamboo poles to the handle of the net. The butterfly net now had a really long handle. She took it back down to the lake.

"Get ready, Juniper!" called Betty as she reached the centre of the lake. "I'm going to set you free today!"

Blundering Buddies

Holding the bathyscope between her knees, she extended it into the water and looked into the viewfinder. "There you are!" she called happily. Then, using both hands, she lowered the net into the water.

The bottle was stuck in the lake's sandy bottom. To loosen it, Betty poked the sand with the net. Finally, she was able to free the bottle. But then it started to drift away!

"Oh bother!" said Betty. "You're getting away from me!" She began swinging her net from left to right, hoping to catch the bottle. With one wild swing, she managed to trap it in the net. She quickly hauled it up. When it bobbed up to the lake's surface she could hardly believe her eyes! There it was, with a tiny sparkling genie inside.

"Good girl, Betty!" said Juniper. "Now, pull the stopper out!"

Betty struggled to pull out the large crystal stopper. Finally, she managed to pull it free. Out popped Juniper, somersaulting with glee!

"Thank you so very much, Betty!" she said. "Now, tell me your wish so that I can fulfil it!"

"Okay! I wish for an amazing invention that

I can present at the science fair tomorrow!" exclaimed Betty.

"Let me see what I can do," said Juniper, twirling her fingers and closing her eyes in concentration.

"Pixies from the fourth dimension,
Provide us with a winning invention!"

Immediately, there was a dazzling cloud of fairy dust and flashes of beautiful golden sparks. Betty blinked. She and Juniper waited with bated breath for the invention to appear. But only a piece of paper fluttered on to the raft. Written on it were the words 'WINNING INVENTION'.

"Oh no!" said Juniper. "I seem to have blundered again! I'm just like you, Betty. I can't seem to do anything right!"

Betty grinned, for she had understood what the words on the paper meant. She hugged Juniper with glee. "No, silly! You have already made my wish come true. Look at this amazing bathyscope, raft and net. I have already made some amazing scientific objects!"

"That's brilliant!" said Juniper excitedly. "They will love your raft and bathyscope at the science fair!"

At the science exhibition the next day, Betty stood proudly next to the raft, bathyscope and net that she had made.

When the judges came to her exhibit, they were very impressed at the strong raft, the clever net and the wonderful bathyscope. "This looks like a very clever object," said one of the judges. "But I'm not sure what it is! Can you tell me what a bathyscope does?"

"It's an Underwater Treasure Finder," replied Betty with a smile. The judges laughed

in delight at Betty's cleverness, understanding immediately how it worked.

Can you guess who won first prize? That's right. It was Betty! And instead of Blundering Betty, her friends started calling her Brilliant Betty!

As for Juniper the genie, she rushed home with a great big smile on her face. To her surprise, everyone had missed her immensely.

Tanglebeard was the first to visit her. "Juniper, bless you!" he roared happily. "I thought you had moved away."

"Oh, I could never leave this dear little place for good," replied Juniper. "But aren't you cross with me for putting a foot in your beard?"

"Not at all," said Tanglebeard. "I was the life and soul of the party. Many people had beards much longer than mine, but mine was the only one with a foot sticking out of it."

"I'm very happy for you," said Juniper. "But it was still a mistake. Besides, Dame Daffodil…"

"Dame Daffodil is as fit as ever!" exclaimed Tanglebeard. "Thanks to you, she learnt to walk without her stick, and her legs got better and stronger. Isn't that wonderful?"

Juniper was speechless. She could hardly believe how everything had worked out, despite all the mistakes she had made. "I guess I'm not such a blunderer after all!" she said, filling with confidence.

And that was exactly how Juniper's magic worked – it didn't grant what you wanted. Instead, it gave you what you needed. So, if things don't always go your way, think about Juniper. Maybe things will turn out for the better.

The Leprechaun's Shoes

Neil was a very smart boy. He was the best at almost everything at school. He was the best in most of his classes; he could sing exceptionally well, and he could solve maths problems faster than anyone else. The only thing that Neil wasn't good at was sport. He wasn't fast, or good at catching or throwing. The boy who was best at sport was called Sean.

Sean was tall, strong and very nimble. He could run faster than all the other boys. He was terrific at football and no one could beat him at tennis. But although Sean was a great sportsman, he was really quite a dreadful boy. He was rude and unpleasant to everyone. He was awful to poor Neil. He would bully him, tease him and make life unhappy for him, and encouraged the other children to tease him about how slow he ran.

The Leprechaun's Shoes

So Neil simply stayed away from Sean. He would play in the woods, his only company being Orla, his beautiful golden retriever dog.

Orla loved Neil very much, and he loved her, too. Orla loved running around and being outdoors. After school was finished for the day, Neil would collect Orla from his house. He would bring treats for her and the two of them would stroll around the village or play a game of fetch in the park. Neil would also often take her into the nearby woods to explore.

One day, Neil and Orla set off for a trip to the woods. Neil brought a snack for himself and some scraps of meat for Orla. As they got closer to the woods, Orla's ears pricked up and she started barking loudly.

"Here, Orla," said Neil, placing the meat on the ground. "Finish your food first. Then we can play!"

But Orla ignored the food completely. She pranced around Neil, sniffing at the floor and barking occasionally at something in the distance.

"Can you smell something, Orla?" Neil asked her. "Well, all right, let's go and see what it is!" Picking up the meat and wrapping it back up in brown paper, he followed Orla as she led him deeper into the woods.

The golden dog ran in front of Neil, stopping at intervals to let him catch up. Eventually she stopped running and stopped at the foot of a large tree, sniffing and barking at it.

"What's here?" asked Neil, scratching his head. "Is it an animal?" But there was nothing on the ground. Orla was looking up the tree, trying to climb it.

That's when Neil saw what she saw. "My goodness!" he cried. "I think there's a little tree house up there!"

Orla could not climb such a big, sturdy tree. Even Neil himself found it hard to find a way up to the little wooden house. Orla watched as Neil began to climb, holding on to the grooves and notches in the bark. At one point his foot slid and his shoe tore on a piece of wood. The shoe slipped off his foot and fell to the ground. Neil's heart began to thump.

He regained his footing and kicked off his other shoe, too. As he climbed, the trunk became more and more slippery, but just when

The Leprechaun's Shoes

he thought his strength was about to fail him, Neil reached the part where the trunk gave way to the branches. Thankfully, the branches made climbing easier, and Neil was able to scramble quickly up to reach the tree house.

The tiny log cabin was balanced across four or five thick, flat branches of the tree. The door was closed tight and there were curtains drawn at each of the little windows. Nobody answered when Neil knocked, but when he pushed on the door, it opened without any resistance.

Neil walked nervously into the tree house. Despite being a little short for his age, he had to crouch to fit inside. It was a simple room with no furniture apart from a small stool in the corner. On the stool sat a tiny old man dressed in a green hooded apron. He seemed to be making a pair of shoes and looked rather cross.

"Hello," said Neil. "I'm sorry for coming in without being invited. But I was just so curious!"

"Dratted children," mumbled the man. "Always meddling in everyone else's business!"

The Leprechaun's Shoes

Neil flushed. He had not meant to disturb the man. He was about to leave quietly when he saw the shoes that the man was making.

"Please, sir," said Neil. "Would you lend me a pair of shoes? Mine ripped and fell off while I was climbing up."

"You tiresome boy!" snapped the man. "Do you think I am a shoe factory? And now you're stuck here. How will you climb down in your socks? Silly, silly, silly…" He went on muttering to himself.

Neil was in quite a fix! How would he climb down? It was already getting dark. Orla was waiting for him at the foot of the tree.

"What am I going to do?" he said to himself, quite worried.

"Stop whining!" said the man rudely.

"But I'm not – ouch!" Before Neil could complete his sentence, the man had thrown a pair of shoes at him.

"Try those on for size," said the man. Neil put on the shoes. They were a perfect fit. Neil walked around the small cabin. They felt like they had been made especially for his feet.

"Thank you so much!" said Neil. "I have no

money to give you, but you can have what I brought with me to eat."

Neil rummaged through his bag and produced the apple and sandwich that his mother had packed for him. The little man took them greedily and started to gobble them up.

"I'll consider this food as payment for the shoes," said the man. "Be on your way now, lad. It's getting dark, and I don't want you here any more!"

The boy climbed down the tree expertly. Even though it was very slippery, his new shoes gripped the tree tightly. It took only a few minutes for Neil to clamber back down to Orla.

"Come on, Orla, we'd better get back quickly. It's getting very dark!"

The woods were very dark and Neil could hardly see his way. He felt very thankful for Orla, who seemed to know her way back quite easily. Whenever they started to feel lost, she sniffed around for a second before bringing them back on to the right track.

"I'm exhausted," he thought. "I will

The Leprechaun's Shoes

definitely sleep well tonight!"

When he got home, Neil ate his supper and then fell sound asleep, tired out from his adventure. The next morning, he began to get ready for school. Just as he was about to put on his shoes, he remembered that he had torn one while climbing the tree. He had forgotten all about them after he climbed back down and had left his old shoes behind.

"Oh no," he said. "If mother finds out, she'll be very cross!"

There was no choice but to wear the shoes that the old man in the tree house had given him.

That day, during gym class, the teacher asked them to run a race. Neil's heart sank: he knew he would come last. But as soon as the teacher blew his whistle, Neil shot off at top speed. His legs seemed to be moving on their own! Even he didn't know where his speed was coming from! Before long he crossed the finishing line, leaving all his classmates trailing behind him.

"That was brilliant, Neil!" said the teacher.

"Thank you," said Neil, still in shock. "But

I don't understand how I managed to do it!"

Seeing Neil win a race made Sean very angry. He usually won all the races, as he was the strongest and had the longest legs.

"You cheated, didn't you?" he asked Neil, grabbing his shirt roughly.

"No, I didn't," replied Neil, quietly. "Now let go of me."

"Tell me how you ran so fast," asked Sean, shaking his fist.

"I already told you – I don't know," said Neil, honestly. "But it might have something to do with these shoes…"

Neil told Sean the entire story of how Orla had led him to the tree where he found the little man's house. On hearing this, Sean grew extremely jealous.

"Now it's my turn to meet that funny little man," he said. "I'll go up the tree after school and get him to make some shoes for me. You have to come with me."

Neil felt too scared to say no. "Okay," said Neil. "But we'll have to take my dog, Orla, with us. She'll make sure we don't get lost."

Later that night, Sean turned up at Neil's

house and they made their way to the woods, with Orla in tow. Orla barked in excitement.

"Be quiet!" he shouted. "Take us to the tree house."

Orla's tail dropped. With a small whimper, she turned away, leading Sean and Neil into the heart of the woods. Soon enough, they reached the tall tree. Sean looked up and spotted the tree house hidden among the branches.

"Aha! We've found it," he said to himself gleefully. He started to climb slowly and steadily. Neil didn't want to rip his new shoes, so he waited at the foot of the tree with Orla. By the time he reached the tree house, it was already getting dark. He barged into the little house without knocking. Sure enough, he saw the little old man sitting in the corner.

"Hey, you!" said Sean, imperiously. "I'm here to get a pair of shoes like the ones you made for that boy yesterday. But they should be much stronger and faster than the ones you gave him, do you hear?"

"Ha!" the man chuckled. "Have I nothing else to do? I'm busy enough! Go away!"

But Sean didn't budge. "I won't leave until I have the shoes," he said.

"You can wait all night, then!" snarled the man.

Sean took out his food and began to feast on it. His bag was packed with buttered scones, moist cucumber sandwiches and fresh strawberries with cream. And to wash it all down, he had a big bottle of ginger beer.

The little man stared at the food. "Give me some of your food to pay for my services," he said. "Then I will think about doing as you ask."

"All right, then," said Sean. He rummaged through his satchel and pulled out a single strawberry. It was the smallest one of the

lot, and was shrivelled up and starting to rot. "Here you go," he said, tossing the strawberry to the man.

Catching it deftly, the man looked at the strawberry between his fingers for a moment. The ghost of a sly smile crept onto his lips. He tossed the strawberry into his mouth and gulped it down without even chewing.

"I'll make your shoes now," said the man, much to Sean's excitement. But the boy didn't realise that the shoemaker was no ordinary man. He was a leprechaun! These little creatures were known to be very shrewd and tricky. He had made Neil some top-quality shoes because Neil had been polite and offered him some food. But Sean was going to get a different sort of surprise!

The leprechaun tinkered around with a few strips of leather and fashioned a pair of shoes in just a few minutes. He tossed them over to Sean.

Sean grabbed them eagerly. Without a word of thanks, he put on the shoes and climbed down the tree. But the shoes didn't have a good grip at all. He slipped dangerously down the tree and fell hard onto the forest floor.

"Ow!" Sean howled. His hands and knees were scraped and bleeding. Neil was a nice boy and despite Sean's bullying, he held out his hand and helped Sean get to his feet. Sean felt very confused. He couldn't understand why he wasn't able to climb down the tree with ease. He didn't suspect that the leprechaun shoemaker had tricked him!

The next day, Sean felt very excited. There was going to be an important race that afternoon. He put on his new shoes and set off for school.

Soon it was time for the race.

"I'm going to beat you all!" he boasted to the other children in his class. "Just watch me!"

But as soon as the race began, Sean could barely run. He kept slipping and running in the opposite direction. "I don't understand!" he said to himself. "Are these shoes jinxed?"

Neil, on the other hand, was able to run faster than ever. He was delighted. It was as if Sean and he had swapped places! Just then, he realised what the old man must have done. He

must have made Sean some bad shoes!

"He must be a leprechaun," thought Neil. "How silly of me not to have noticed straight away! I've read that leprechauns sometimes play tricks on naughty people!"

That afternoon, Neil decided to take some food to the leprechaun as a thank-you for his shoes. While leprechauns could be very mischievous, he had certainly been generous in Neil's time of need!

Neil went home and packed a delicious picnic. His mother gave him a basket filled with meat pies, tossed salad, macaroons, fruit, fizzy strawberry soda, and freshly baked banana bread.

"Thank you, Mum," said Neil. "You know how Orla loves to bite into a crusty pie!"

But when Orla and Neil went back to the tree that evening, they found that the tree house was gone! Neil felt a little sad, until he realised that the leprechaun must have shown up when he most needed some magical help. Just then, Neil saw a strange twinkling in the distance. It lasted for only a minute before disappearing. To Neil, it almost looked as though two beady little eyes were winking at him mischievously. He waved in the direction of the lights, and then turned back to go home.

From that day onwards, Sean stopped being nasty to Neil. And as for Neil? He became the star sportsman of the school. All thanks to a strange little leprechaun in a tiny tree house.